A SEASONAL *P*URSUIT

A
*Regency Christmas Brides
Novel*

by

REBECCA CONNOLLY

To the Holiday Romance lovers of any time period. May you always have the twinkling lights, hot cocoa, and perfect music for those moments you crave.

And to me, quite honestly. This book and this romance was entirely for me.

Want to hear about future releases and upcoming events for Rebecca Connolly?
Sign up for the monthly Wit and Whimsy at:

www.rebeccaconnolly.com

CHAPTER 1
London, December 1814

Rose Portman loved her family.

Loved was a rather loose term, in her mind, meaning she tolerated them in appropriate doses, would defend them to anyone, and found them to be the least objectionable people in Society. They were the only people who truly knew her, which was a mixture of good and evil, and the only ones who did not gossip about her—mostly. She did not *think* her sisters gossiped about her, but there were no certainties there.

All of this did not mean, however, that her family did not also confuse, torment, aggravate, and downright exasperate to an excessive degree, sometimes for an extended period of time, and sometimes only limited to specific persons.

Her great-aunt was one such person, having been an eccentric most of her life, and she had gathered four of her siblings' offspring into one room to meet with a solicitor, reason unknown.

Rose had had quite enough of unknowns and speculation in her life and now preferred only the most comfortable and clear styles of life and manner. Being nine-and-twenty years of age without a single offer of marriage, or true desire to have one, gave her such liberty of tastes. And when her time could be much better spent with the boring combination of a tome of ancient literature and a lukewarm cup of tea instead of sitting here in this stuffy room, she was bound to be a trifle irritable.

Her curiosity was piqued, but only in the mildest sense. She was the only female in the room, sharing this boredom with three of her male cousins, all of whom she tolerated perfectly well, and none of them had any ideas why they were here, if their expressions were anything to go by.

That was an interesting family trait: clear emotional expressions. At least among each other. Which meant there were very few secrets among them.

More's the pity.

She drummed her fingers on the arms of her chair, trying to ignore the rather deafening sounds of the long clock in the corner of the room. She cast her eyes down the row of her cousins, and as she suspected, their faces were a veritable mirror of annoyed boredom.

What a unifying moment for their family.

Alden, down on the far end, glanced over, and Colin, next to him, leaned forward. "Do you know what this is about?"

Alden shook his head. "I do not. I was hoping you did."

They both looked at Richard, who sat on Rose's immediate left, then at her, and in unison, Rose and Richard shrugged.

Beautiful family coordination. What a triumph.

The office door opened then, drawing their attention towards it at once. A thin face with spectacles peeked around it, sheepishly smiling at them. "I apologize for the wait. Do come in."

The cousins rose fluidly, two of them muttering under their breath as they traipsed into the room. A large desk took up most of the space, and a short man with a thin face stood on the working side of it, gesturing for them all to take seats. There were only three chairs, so Alden moved to the window while the rest sat.

Rose eyed the desk as she situated herself, the extreme tidiness of the papers on its surface boding well for the man of business.

"Allow me to introduce myself," the man announced with a smile. "My name is Mr. Davidson. I am Lady Edith Walker's solicitor."

Considering they'd all had that general idea already, and the man's name was one of those on the sign of the place, this was not much of a revelation.

"Why are we here?" Colin demanded without much patience.

Colin had never been one for patience.

Nonplussed, Mr. Davidson continued. "I'm afraid that I am the bearer of some bad news. Lady Edith is dying."

A gasp escaped Rose, quite unexpectedly, but it could not be helped. Aunt Edith was the sort of person who was destined to outlive several generations, and though she was of a certain age, death was not something that had ever seemed likely to perturb the woman.

"Oh dear," Alden muttered, looking a trifle winded. "How much longer does Aunt Edith have?"

"It is hard to say," Mr. Davidson told them all, somber faced and sympathetic.

Rose only managed a stray blink or two, still trying to process the fact of Aunt Edith dying soon. The woman might be eccentric, but she was still family, and family gatherings would not be the same without trying to avoid being trapped into conversation alone with her. Nor without the particularly detailed gossip she could spout on any member of the family, of Society, or of historical figures. More than one glass of Madeira loosened Aunt Edith's tongue for all the world, and Uncle George did so enjoy plying her excessively with drink when he could.

Who would be the center of all information for them now?

Mr. Davidson cleared his throat, drawing Rose back to the present. "I requested this visit because Lady Edith wrote each one of you a letter. She would like you to read them here, and I am available to answer any questions you may have." He handed out letters to each of them and returned to his seat, watching them all with remarkable calm.

A letter from a dying relative. That seemed positively morbid, and Rose, certainly not Aunt Edith's favorite niece, found herself filled with as much dread as she did curiosity.

Still, it seemed in poor taste to refuse a dying woman's letter. She unfolded the paper and began scanning the lines quickly.

My darling Rose,

If all has gone accordingly, you have just been informed that I am not long for this world. But that has only spurred me to be rather blunt with you, dear girl, and to not spare your feelings.

I wish for you to marry, not for comforts or status or expectation, but for love. Your sisters, bless them, have made admirable matches, but they bear the sort of demeanors that would make affable marriages with nearly anyone. You are far more difficult, prickly, and particular, which would make a love match the greater victory. You are capable of a great love, if you will set your mind and, more importantly, your heart on it. I am determined you shall have it, and have arranged matters accordingly.

There is a cottage in the Cotswolds, just outside the charming village of Bibury, that I will bequeath to you, along with a generous stipend to maintain it. It bears five bedchambers, a library, two parlors, a healthy garden, and its own stables. Beechwood Lodge and all that accompanies it will be yours if you meet my terms.

You will attend a Christmas house party hosted by my dear friend

Lady Standhope at her estate in York, Fairview. You must make yourself a match of affection and love from those in attendance at this party and become engaged before the end of Twelfth Night. Lady Standhope knows of these terms and will be sure to offer any assistance you require as well as keep me informed.

If my health and the weather permits, I shall trespass upon my dear friend's kindness to meet your intended before the end of the party.

All my love,

Aunt Edith

"Oh my actual days…" Rose breathed.

"Scotland?" Alden bleated from his perch at the window. He argued with the solicitor a moment while Rose's ears began to ring and burn with embarrassment and indignity.

Difficult? Prickly? Particular? She was nothing of the sort! She simply was who she was, and her sisters were of a more smiley temperament! Anybody would appear as a crone by comparison! Her sister Marina bore actual lines on her face, even at her young age, from excessive smiling!

"Aunt Edith cannot be serious," Richard practically pleaded, finally speaking and breaking through the haze about Rose's ears. "She wants me to wed before Twelfth Night? That is little more than a month."

Rose closed her eyes, shaking her head. The length of time wasn't her main concern; it was the entire prospect.

"That is correct. And Lady Edith is aware of the time restraint." Mr. Davidson still appeared sympathetic, but Rose was convinced he was also secretly laughing at them.

Devil take the man. And devil take Aunt Edith, while he was at it.

"It is impossible!" Richard insisted.

Alden huffed, folding his letter roughly. "At least you don't have to marry a chit from a small village in Scotland."

Rose turned in her chair, raising a brow at him. "What of me? I am supposed to attend a house party for Christmas."

All three of her cousins seemed to scoff at once. "A house party?" Alden repeated, only very slightly smiling. "That doesn't sound like you."

Rose nodded, eyes widening, and turned back around, glancing at the other two.

Poor Colin seemed rather pale and beyond words. Richard continued to shake his head.

At least they were all in this stupidity together. But would they do as Aunt Edith asked?

"That coach will not be necessary," Alden announced, straightening. "I have no intention of going to Scotland for Christmas."

Mr. Davidson had the gall to appear shocked. "But…"

"I agree with what Richard said," Alden overrode with a raised hand, stopping the man. "What our aunt Edith is asking of us is impossible." He moved to the door and glanced back at them all with a nod. "I wish you luck, but I want nothing to do with this ruse." And then he was gone.

"That was a very Alden thing to do," Rose muttered to herself.

"Impossible," Richard whispered as he looked over his own letter. "Absolutely impossible."

Rose looked at Colin, who still hadn't said a word. "Colin?"

He exhaled slowly and met her eyes. "It's a lot of money. And we all know I need it. I just don't know."

That was fair, but Rose need not feel the same pressure. She looked at her letter and twisted her lips. What Aunt Edith was offering was exactly the sort of situation Rose wanted for herself, but she had also recently struck a bargain with her father that if she remained unmarried until the age of five and thirty, she would receive her dowry for herself. Ten thousand pounds could buy a cottage anywhere, and a comfortable life, if she were prudent with her funds.

And it avoided the issue of marriage entirely.

But to get what she wanted now instead of later, even if she had to marry... Distant marriages happened all the time, even if they had started out well enough. She could certainly find a good match with someone who could pretend to be in love with her for her aunt's purposes, and then she could live at the cottage while her husband lived anywhere else and did as he chose. Who wouldn't love such an arrangement?

Shaking her head, Rose stood and folded her letter, tucking it into her reticule. "Mr. Davidson, I will consider my aunt's offer. I cannot make this decision without thought. Will two days be acceptable?"

Mr. Davidson seemed a trifle relieved she was not also going to storm out. "Of course, Miss Portman. I will wait for your answer."

She nodded and walked by Richard and Colin, patting each on the head as she passed like they were part of some bizarre game.

After all, they were.

Leaving the room, then the building, Rose climbed into her father's carriage, her thoughts awhirl as she was returned home.

She hated being social. Despised incessant chatter at social gatherings. Rarely found anyone worth conversing with. But what if...?

There was no harm in trying, surely. If she went to this party, there was the possibility she could find someone to engage in this scheme with, even if love or affection were not present. And if she could not, she had her father's promise to fall back on.

And spending a Christmas away from her sisters meant that no one would ask her awkward questions. Her nieces and nephews would miss her, of course, but she might have to risk it.

Her dream of a cottage life and solitude might be closer than six years hence, and her independence was too tempting a prospect to ignore.

Aunt Edith was pulling all of their strings in this, and Rose was, unfortunately, ripe for such pulling.

CHAPTER 2

Webb Rixton sighed with contentment as he entered his home after a brisk ride in the winter air. There was nothing like such a ride to invigorate the spirits and make one feel remarkably alive when the world around him was going dormant for a season. Not many gentlemen would willingly ride in the cold, but he would. So long as one invested in a well-made woolen coat and bundled up accordingly, there was nothing terrible about the endeavor.

And he was desperate to get in as many such rides as he could before the snows came. After the frigid temperatures and mountainous snows of last year, he could not take any chances.

He always felt a little hemmed in when the weather began to hamper his activities. It was a rather elevated annoyance, considering what his tenants had to contend with, but he had always done his best to ensure that all of them had as many comforts as possible. Repairs were timely, wood was in ample supply, and foodstuffs were given to those without means to support themselves accordingly. Any complaints were quickly addressed, and always would be.

Because of such efficiency, however, he had several

stretches of time where there was absolutely nothing to do, and when riding was also denied him...

It was a most inconvenient state of existence.

Webb nodded warmly as his capable and nearly of an age butler approached him. "Crosby."

Crosby bowed. "My lord, your sister is here."

In one fluid motion, Webb turned on his heel and started for the door through which he had just entered.

"Not so fast, Webb! I've seen you!" that same sister's voice cried out from the drawing room to his left.

Sighing and not bothering to hide his grimace, Webb stopped and let his shoulders droop in defeat. Then he trudged over to the drawing room, wishing his boots were covered in mud so he might have an excuse to not enter.

No such luck.

Forcing the polite sort of smile one saved for one's inconveniently arrived family members, Webb gave his younger sister a half bow of acknowledgement. "Emily."

Emily, dark haired and dark eyed like himself, smiled over her cup of tea. "Come. Sit."

Webb didn't move. "Not in this condition, thank you. I need to change."

"You need to listen to what I have to say," his sister corrected, motioning for him to sit again.

"You are becoming more and more like Mother every day," he informed her, still remaining in place.

Her expression turned scolding. "How dare you. What will Bertram say when I tell him?"

"Your husband will agree with me, as he sees you as clearly as I do. The problem with Bertram is that he likes what he sees." Webb batted his lashes teasingly.

Emily huffed and set her teacup and saucer down on the nearby table. "Webb, I've come to discuss Christmas."

"Excellent," he countered. "I think we should celebrate it."

She ignored him. "Kitty and Pierce are getting older, and so are you."

Any playfulness or desire for banter fled from Webb at once, his chest beginning to turn as cold as the air of his ride. His children were three and four, respectively, and the only reason his sister would be bringing up their ages, and his own, was to remind him of the family position.

Everyone agreed that Webb should not be alone.

Even Webb agreed on this. However, Webb, being the one who would need to act, did not see the need to hasten the change. It had only been eighteen months since Mary had died, and while the loss was no longer sharp enough to steal his breath, it still ached in several corners of his soul.

No number of brisk rides would chase those shadows away.

"What does this have to do with Christmas?" Webb asked in a softer voice. "Have they said anything?"

His children occasionally asked their governess to help them send letters to their cousins, and secrets had come out a time or two in those letters, particularly if they did not want to broach a subject with Webb.

They didn't fear him, or anything so horrific. They had simply learned the beauty of someone else making suggestions to their father rather than doing the task themselves.

Webb prided himself on being a very active sort of father, especially since Mary's death, and took great pride in being as playful as possible so they might have some semblance of a childhood, even without their mother.

Last Christmas, Mary's loss had been particularly acute, but there had been a great deal of snow, which allowed Webb to distract them with wintery adventures as well as the presents he felt Mary would wish for them. He might have given too much, but he had been willing to risk that in compensation.

"No, they haven't," Emily assured him with a warm smile. "At least, not that my three have confessed. Webb, please sit."

He actually considered joining her in this confined space, now that he knew his children were not writing their cousins about concerns over Christmas. If that was the case, there might be something worth listening to here.

And he could always get up and leave if he reached his tolerance for intervention soon. It was only his sister, after all. If she hadn't gotten mortally offended by him yet, she wouldn't do so now.

With a hesitant look, he took the nearest chair, not reaching for any tea or biscuits, as doing so might encourage her to draw this out, whatever it was.

Emily kept her eyes on him, her mouth pinching at the corners. "Webb, I want you to accept Lady Standhope's invitation to her holiday house party."

Webb blinked at his sister in surprise. "How can I possibly do that?" he asked her. "The entire family comes here for Christmas, including our brothers. Do you think Fred is going to accept my being absent while you lot run about Downing House being festive? Or Bash, for that matter? And what kind of state will I find the place in with those two idiots roaming about without proper adult supervision?"

"Erm, I would be here," Emily reminded him as she fetched her tea once more.

"You and Bertram would clearly be the only ones responsible for the children, as you are the only others who have any," Webb retorted, sitting back and crossing one boot over his knee.

Emily sniffed, which told him she had no other defense for herself. "Mother would be here. She'd never spend Christmas alone at the dower house."

Webb snorted without reserve. "Since when has Mother

ever properly managed Fred and Bash? How do you think they got that way?"

"Fine!" Emily rolled her eyes, sipping her tea rather loudly for a lady. "Fine. Then go to the house party and only stay some of the evenings. You live four miles away, not twenty. It is a simple enough thing."

"Why stay at all if I live so close?" Webb inquired mildly, now more interested in provoking his sister with questions than in the idea she proposed. "Surely I will be more comfortable in my own bed."

Emily glared over the rim of her teacup. "Because it is a poor guest who leaves a ball early just for the sake of preferring his own pillows."

"I hate balls. I always leave them early."

"You haven't been to a ball since you've come out of mourning, so it's been at least a year and a half that you've even attended one."

Webb stared at her for a long moment, less angry than stung. "You know why."

Emily set her teacup on her knee gently, lowering her eyes for a moment. "Yes, I do. I am not blaming you for it, only stating the facts. And I am certainly not saying that you need to marry, Webb. Kitty and Pierce need a mother figure, but that is not an incentive I want you to keep in your head. I would be furious and disappointed if that were your reason for taking a wife."

"Good," he grunted as he looked out of the window, pretending he was pensive.

He knew she was right, which was as galling as it was uncomfortable. His children did need a mother figure in their lives, and he wanted one for them. He also missed the companionship that his wife had provided, and knew that, if he chose wisely, another wife could fill that void. But Mary had been his childhood sweetheart, and the idea that someone else could

13

take her place was impossible. That any other woman would suit him as well felt like a betrayal. That love in any shade could find his heart once more felt like foolishness. That he could feel as alive as he once had seemed wistful.

But he wanted it. He wanted it to be possible, to be true, to be tangible...

Good heavens, did he actually have hope? He hadn't spent any time really considering the idea, but now that his sister had put a voice to it, something seemed to be fluttering against the weight in his chest. Not quite flying, but certainly straining to do so.

"I just think you need to start being social once more," Emily was saying, bringing his attention out of himself and back to her. "And do not tell me that you have been associating with your tenants and some men of business, because you know that is not what I mean."

Webb fought a smile. His sister knew him well. "I've also been to the village quite a lot," he pointed out.

The look she gave him—one their mother had clearly passed on—was severe.

He held up his hands quickly in surrender before folding them in his lap and heaving a sigh. "Oh, perhaps you are right."

"I am?" She blinked her wide eyes as though she could not believe what she was hearing.

Webb grinned freely now. "Are you more shocked that I have stopped arguing or that I admitted you are right?"

"Honestly, both." She took a long sip of her tea before speaking again. "I had an entire speech prepared to give for when you would begin to consider the idea, but you've skipped that step entirely. I didn't expect you to admit that I was right until the very end, if at all today."

"It is nice to know I am not yet so predictable." He leaned his head back against his chair, looking up at the ceiling. "So how would it work? Would you and Bertram entertain the children while I am away? What would you have planned that I would miss out on?"

Emily shook her head as she set her tea down. "The boys would come in on St. Thomas's Day or so, certainly before Christmas Eve. We'll decorate Downing House with the children on Christmas Eve, and meet you at church on Christmas Day, perhaps. Then we could all come back here for a large Christmas luncheon so the children don't feel as though they have missed out on a feast, and you can return to Fairview for Christmas dinner, as I am certain Lady Standhope will have a great feast and a ball planned for the night. Then you might return here on St. Stephen's Day and we can all give out gifts to the tenants and servants. The boys will go on a fox hunt with Bertram and some neighbors, perhaps. And then we might have an evening of games just for the children, and you can come home for that, depending on Lady Standhope's scheduling. And Twelfth Night, I am positive, will be a night for you to remain at Fairview."

Webb was watching her now, brow furrowed. "Two weeks," he calculated, needing to make absolutely certain that he understood his sister perfectly. "You want me to be in and out of my own home during the holiday season for two weeks just to be social with my neighbor, who is hosting some grand and festive house party. Miss out on making memories with my children, who are now at an age where memories remain."

Emily exhaled irritably. "You see, this is one of the arguments I anticipated you making earlier."

"Well, it is a legitimate concern!" he protested, flinging his hands out. "I want to be a present father, not an absent one!"

"Then allow me to get a proposed schedule from Lady Standhope, and we will create our own based on hers!" Emily yelled back, spilling a bit of tea on her skirts. She brushed the liquid off in a huff and set the tea down on the table again before folding her hands together in front of her, her eyes fixed on Webb. "You need your spark back, Webb. Your children adore you, and that will not change. And it is not as though we are going to be occupied every minute of every day. You know how leisurely we all are at times."

He had to smile at that. His siblings were famed for never eating breakfast before eleven, and his sister almost never did so out of bed, and they were firmly rooted in these behaviors when they were all together. A poor tendency to stay up late and laugh together, if not generally misbehave, was likely to blame, but his brothers might have developed a bit of wickedness all their own that also contributed.

Emily clicked her tongue softly. "I want you to be active in your life again. You are not the sort of man best suited to being a recluse, and you are certainly not the sort to live the rest of your life alone. If you want a wife again someday, and I think you do, you will need to get out again. And I promise you, the longer you spend alone, the harder it will be to change."

He would be lying if he claimed he was not moved by her words, nor by the impassioned way she said them. His sister had always been bold and frank, but she was also remarkably caring and observant. It was very like her to see something that he knew was there but had chosen to ignore, and for her to say something that was exactly right. He rarely told her so, but there it was.

A Christmas house party was undoubtedly a better excuse to be social than any one set in the summer, when he had more work to do on his land. And everyone was bound to be in high spirits during such a festive time, so it would be easier for him to be around them. He was generally a sociable person, but it had been quite a while…

He was running out of excuses, and if his sister's triumphant smile was anything to go by, she knew it, too.

"If you can get the schedule from Lady Standhope," he said

slowly, "and arrange activities so I have quality time with the children *and* convince Mother to remain here the entire time I am gone, then I will accept."

"Done," Emily agreed with haste and a firmness he instantly hated. She pushed to her feet and pulled her gloves on. "I will be in touch." And with a flounce of her skirts, she strode out of the room.

Webb stared at her now empty chair, and wondered if he might have just sold his soul for the holidays.

CHAPTER 3

The only thing that kept Rose from a completely sour mood as she arrived at Fairview was the spectacular sight it was and its rather perfect situation.

The roads had been dreadful, as one might have expected in the weather, and her head ached abominably from the swaying and discomfort of the carriage. Her eyes were tired of the passing scenery, lovely though Yorkshire was, and the cramped space of the carriage felt rather pokey after so many hours. She had not slept well at the inn, and the maid she had brought with her had fixed her hair so tightly this morning that her neck positively throbbed with tension.

Her mother and sisters had insisted upon her using a maid, which Rose had not had to endure for at least six years, saying that it would also make her travel less dangerous, as there would be two of them. Considering Rose was not traveling with a fortune and was far beyond her bloom, the idea that her going anywhere alone was in any way a tempting prospect for villains was laughable, in her mind. But arguing was not an activity she enjoyed, and the squealing, overly cheery suggestions of her sisters lessened when she accepted the minimum. Anna, in particular, had given her a list of benefits a maid would provide her on this trip.

She should never have left her letter from Aunt Edith lying around. Their snooping eyes found it the very next time they took tea at the family London house, and Rose had not had much of a say in anything ever since.

To say that Fairview was a welcome sight would be an understatement. But she had not anticipated the loveliness of it either, which served to lighten her discomfort just enough to cause a smile.

The house itself seemed to extend for miles in either direction, the immaculate stonework shifting from tan to grey in color when the sun ducked behind clouds. Windows dotted the entire lengthy facade, and the details upon the tops of each window and along the surface of the roof were so beautifully gothic that Rose wished she had brought some novels with her for ambience. Columns and stairs and terraces seemed to appear from the oddest portions of the place, and yet flowed with perfect continuity among the style and framework. It was, without a doubt, the grandest house that Rose had ever visited, let alone been invited to.

Suddenly none of this seemed like such a terrible idea after all.

The expansive front drive was filled with carriages, and men, women, and, shockingly enough, children were disembarking from them and starting up the stairs. Everyone was bundled in winter-appropriate travel attire, but the air was not so cold as to be frigid today, which must be a comfort to the parents.

Children at a house party. Why? Who would wish to travel with their children at this time of year? And what in the world were children going to do for two weeks at a strange house with adults who were almost certainly going to be more focused on making merry, making mischief, and in her case, making

19

matches? Children did not belong at house parties, and the fact that Lady Standhope did not seem to agree with that notion made Rose all the more confused about this situation. Family parties, certainly, but a social house party?

Rose had several nieces and nephews and she adored them all—though she much preferred the younger age of children to the alternative—but surely even her sisters would agree that there was a time and place for them in social situations.

What if this was a collection of families that had been invited for Christmas at Fairview and not select individuals or couples who might be influential and like-minded? What if there would be no marriage prospects for Rose among the gathering? What if Aunt Edith was teasing Rose with this scheme and had no intention of her succeeding?

What if she was only teaching her a lesson?

It wasn't such a far-fetched idea. Aunt Edith had always been eccentric, after all, and in her waning years, she could have grown slightly mean-spirited as well as more outspoken. Rose had never offended the woman, as far as she knew, but one could never truly account for the intentions of the superior-minded.

She watched another carriage unload as she waited in the line and felt a wash of relief as two women disembarked, but no children. They were younger than her, which was not surprising, and were clearly sisters by their similar appearances. Neatly dressed, not overly exuberant, and neither of them were waiting for men to get off horses or the like before proceeding into the house.

Spinsters and families, then, if nothing else.

Better than her being singled out and alone.

Rose watched as servants unloaded trunks and boxes from coaches and wagons, proceeding into the house at ground level rather than going up the stairs, and she found herself nodding as she pictured the layout of the estate in her mind. Not that any of it mattered where she was concerned, but it was always interesting for her to understand the way rooms and floors were arranged in country houses. And when a house looked like this, she was even more curious.

She might spend the entire two weeks exploring Fairview instead of looking for a spouse. Her time would probably be better spent doing so, and she would certainly enjoy it more.

A man disembarked from the next carriage, and no woman followed him, nor children. He was perhaps five-and-thirty, and wore the plain, dark clothing of a clergyman.

Always an interesting possibility, a man of the church. She was not particularly religious herself, but she had also learned that not all men of the church were religious either. Some merely appreciated the appearance of piety, some enjoyed a life of service and charity, and some simply needed an occupation that was not as demanding as the army as or as intellectual as the law.

One unmarried man, at least. If he was the only one, her object would be easy enough.

She snorted to herself as her carriage moved closer to the house. As if her aunt would really believe Rose would fall in love with a clergyman or curate.

Why had she made the distinction of marrying for love, or at least affection? Rose was not prone to flights of fancy or feelings of whimsy at her age, especially after her experience in Society. She might never find love or affection, and even when she was younger, it hadn't happened.

Now she was meant to find it in two weeks.

Ridiculous, frivolous notion.

She didn't even know if Aunt Edith had married for love. That might have been something she ought to know, especially if she was taking up the charge the woman had set her. The sheer hypocrisy of demanding she—and her cousins—marry for love if she had not done so herself!

She might have to write a letter to Colin on the subject. He could uncover the truth and possibly release them all from this idiocy. If they held the trump card collectively, Aunt Edith might give way.

After a few more carriages, it was finally Rose's turn to unload, and she took a quick moment to glance down at herself once her feet touched the gravel of the drive. Her coat was a simple grey, but the trim was a deep green and the hem of her skirts matched. Her bonnet also matched, and her hair, apart from making her head ache, did look fetching beneath it, unless she had dislodged something on the drive from the inn.

Perfectly presentable, as her mother would say. That had been all anyone had expected of Rose for the last several years, and she loved the ease of such expectation.

She nodded at her maid—whatever her name was—who began seeing to her bags, and moved towards the stairs, following the same path the other guests had trod. They were not exceptionally long, but there was a full turn in them to reach the first floor of the house, which felt more like a detail that ought to have been reserved for stairs *within* the house rather than without, but Rose was no architect. And the matching set of stairs just opposite her on the other side of the entrance did add some texture to the front façade, she supposed.

Finally mounting the top step and terrace, Rose forced her smile to be more than the simple upward curve of her lips, seeing Lady Standhope just inside the door. She'd never met her before, but the way the grey-haired woman in fine clothing was extending her hands to everyone ahead of Rose seemed to indicate her identity as hostess adequately.

She was taller than Rose had expected, and as plump as was age appropriate, her coloring rosy and her countenance full of good humor. Her voice was a trifle on the trilling side for Rose's taste, but women over the age of fifty could speak however they liked, in her estimation. She personally planned on going rather gravelly in tone when she reached that age, and let people wonder how she had managed to get her voice and throat such a way.

Her smile became rather forced as she dragged her mind back to the present, approaching her hostess with what she hoped was still a perfectly presentable appearance.

"Ah, Miss Portman!" Lady Standhope greeted with the sort of natural effusiveness that one could not dislike. "I was *so* delighted when Lady Edith told me to expect you." She took Rose's hands in both of hers, her hands slightly chilled and well-moisturized. "Now, I don't want you to worry about a thing. I have invited families and friends, but there will be plenty of candidates for you to choose from for your aunt's requirements."

Rose's smile began to make her cheeks ache with its force. "Lady Standhope, I—"

"No, no, no," the older woman interrupted, squeezing her hands tightly. "I will not be hounding you the entire time. I can assure you, my time will be taken up with far too many things. You are to be your own mistress entirely in this endeavor. I shall be available to assist you, should you have need of me, but in this, you will be on your own." She winked and nodded excessively, the dangling baubles among the ribbons of her hair swaying precariously as she did so. "No one likes to be examined every minute of every day, and no romance can flourish when so observed. And even at your age, dear, I do believe in romance. Now, kindly follow Peter here to your rooms. Refresh yourself and rest. We will not officially gather until dinner, which will begin promptly at half four." She gestured towards her right, clearly indicating that Rose was dismissed and should move in that direction, and sure enough, a young and somber faced footman stood there waiting.

Rose curtseyed to Lady Standhope and did as indicated,

wondering if the good lady intended to hold all conversations with herself rather than with those in her company. Time would tell, she supposed.

The thought alone earned her a sigh for herself. It would not do to consider her hostess to be any sort of ridiculous creature, especially if she might need her help to accomplish what Aunt Edith wished. And Lady Standhope did have a delightful home here at Fairview. Surely she had earned the right to be whatever sort of ridiculous she wished to be without being singled out for it.

Up on the second floor, valets, maids, footmen, and guests were going in and out of bedchambers in a flurry of movement up and down the corridor of rooms, not a single creature taking notice of her, nor of each other. There were so many rooms that she was struggling to keep track of how many she had passed and which door led to her chambers among the collection of them. How in the world did Lady Standhope expect to keep up with the names and details of all of them while she hosted them?

None of the children were running about in the corridor, Rose noticed with some relief. She took a few steps closer to her footman/guide. "Are the children in another part of the house, Peter?"

"The families are in the west wing, Miss Portman," Peter informed her with a deferential nod. "A nursery for the children and the parents near enough to wait upon them, if necessary. All in this wing are childless."

Rose nodded, doing her best not to smile, as it would certainly not do to appear pleased.

Even if she was.

"Here is your bedchamber, Miss Portman," Peter said soon after, gesturing to the room at his left, door ajar and beautiful daylight streaming through the windows.

Rose paused before entering, taking a moment to note the

watercolor of dogs at a pond to one side of her door and an ornate looking glass of gold at the other. She would mark her destination by those items, if ever she lost her way.

The room itself was charming, clean, and boasted a marvelous view of the grounds to the north, the dip of a hill in the distance providing something of a vista of the lands beyond. It was a gorgeous piece of England, there was no mistaking it, and even in the dormancy of winter, she could see herself walking a great deal out in such beauty. The temperatures were not so cold, after all, and they were unlikely to receive the snow they had the previous Christmas.

House parties, as she understood it, usually allowed for the guests to do as they pleased during the day, and spending time out of doors when it was fair might just be what she chose to do.

She would, of course, be in the library when the weather prevented outdoor wanderings.

"If you need anything, Miss Portman," Peter was saying, bringing her back to the moment, "do let your maid know and she will inform one of us."

Rose turned back to him and began removing her bonnet, not having to force her smile now. "Thank you, Peter." She tossed the bonnet to one side and nodded at him.

He bowed and departed, leaving her alone in the room, though the bustle from the corridor was certainly audible. Her trunk sat in the corner and the armoire sat open, though none of her belongings currently hung within. Her maid must be somewhere below stairs or still trying to find her way up. It was an extraordinary distance to go, so she wouldn't blame the poor girl. She imagined the servants were taking note of the plans for the evening so as to dress their masters and mistresses accordingly, but Rose wasn't about to occupy her thoughts with such clutter.

She wanted a nap, and she suspected, based on the tall and

rather fluffy-looking bed nearby, that she would be able to do so better here than she had in several days.

With a barely restrained squeal, she ran to the bed and jumped upon the surface, flinging herself upon it with a splayed inelegance that quickly morphed into a deep sigh of comfortable satisfaction.

It was as heavenly as she had hoped it would be.

"Sorry to intrude, but can I just say…?"

Rose squeezed her eyes shut, wincing dramatically before pushing herself up on her hands and craning around to look at the door.

Tall, dark, and handsome stood there, somewhere in his thirties, dressed like the perfect country gentleman, and he was smiling ruefully at her.

Clearly, he had seen the whole thing.

There was no excuse to be made, so Rose only cocked her head, raising a brow in spite of her flaming cheeks.

His smile deepened. "I was thinking of doing the same thing in my room. Was it worth it?"

It was impossible for her to say if he was teasing her or not, but she was long past pretending at anything with anyone anymore.

"Yes," Rose told him simply. "Thrilling, and now I look forward to my rest more than ever."

He nodded precisely once. "Excellent. I shall go and do the same. I shall let you know of my experience at dinner." And then he was gone.

Rose blinked at the empty doorway, then lay back down, grabbed a nearby pillow, and screamed out her mortification into its depths.

CHAPTER 4

Webb hadn't expected to be looking forward to dinner his first night at Fairview, but after having seen the woman break all protocol and fling herself upon her bed like an eager child, he was rather curious to see her again. He could tell she had been mortified at being seen, both by her red cheeks and her defiant stare afterwards, which told him this behavior wasn't in her usual nature, so he'd kept the conversation short. A more polite man might have ignored the entire thing, and certainly wouldn't have spoken of it with the subject, but he found himself unable to resist.

Her response had been fairly acerbic, and something about that delighted him.

More than that, he'd done exactly as he'd said and thrown himself on the bed in his own room and enjoyed quite a good rest, despite not having near as long of a distance to travel as any of the other guests in the house.

It wasn't his first experience of flinging himself on a bed. On the contrary, he did so almost regularly with his children. But his children were not here, which was what made his behavior this time all the more extraordinary.

Lady Standhope was keeping them all in this drawing room-turned-anteroom until the dinner arrangements she had organized were fully prepared for them, and based on the number of guests still trickling in from other parts of the house, she was wise to not keep to her prompt timing of half four. Webb stayed mostly away from the gathering, despite not having any particular aversion to those present, mostly to avoid becoming anyone's fast favorite. He would be dismayed to find that a poor young lady had set her cap at him based on first impressions, only to have them disappointed when he made no pursuit of courtship.

There were very few problems with being a friendly, congenial sort, but that was one of them. He'd faced it briefly before he and Mary had wed, but so long as he had stayed local and avoided extended Society, the misunderstandings were minimal. And in the time since Mary's death…

Well, he hadn't been out in Society, let alone among those who were seeking a spouse.

Not that he was seeking one now.

He simply wanted to keep things simple and clear.

"Lord Downing, what a delight to see you here."

Webb managed a faint smile as he turned to the approaching figure of the local curate. "Mr. Alchurch, isn't it?"

Alchurch bowed with a ready smile. "It is, sir. Very kind of you to remember."

"You've been at the parsonage for four months now, I believe," Webb countered. "It would be rather a blight on my character, and indeed, my immortal soul, if I did not know your name." He sobered a little. "Has Mr. Fenwick recovered from his gout?"

"Not yet, my lord. I fear I will be taking over the sermons for the foreseeable future." Alchurch shrugged slightly, his hands spreading out. "I don't mind. Advent is a wonderful time to be preaching, and the congregation is far more attentive."

Webb nodded in understanding, secretly quite pleased with Alchurch taking over the sermons. He was more lively and pleasant, and also understood the benefits of brevity and moderation in his messages. Poor Fenwick was becoming far too prone to doddering, drudgery, and duration, not to mention entirely unaware of the somnolent nature of the congregation throughout his words.

How the man managed not to hear the snores emanating from parishioners, Webb would never know.

"Lord Downing, Mr. Alchurch," Lady Standhope greeted with her bubbling laugh, sweeping in between the men. "Forgive my intrusion into your conversation, but I must have you both meet Miss Portman. She is a delightful creature and would be good company at dinner." She gestured behind her, forcing both men to turn.

Webb bit back a grin, for there stood the bed-flopping woman from earlier, looking rather lovely in a gown of a green velvet bodice and white skirts, her dark hair pulled back almost severely, though curls at her temples and ears set off the severity nicely.

Her bright blue eyes were wide on Lady Standhope, her lips pinched, and Webb wondered which part of her description Miss Portman objected to.

Still, Webb and Alchurch bowed, and Miss Portman curtseyed, and somehow, in the midst of that, Lady Standhope had moved on.

Miss Portman watched the now distant woman who was their hostess with a hint of exasperation before turning her attention to Webb and Alchurch. "I should warn you, gentlemen, that I am neither delightful nor good company, according to most that know me. Lady Standhope is generous, but she does not know me, so unfortunately her word cannot be trusted where I am concerned."

Alchurch smiled and made room for her to join their conversation. "I am sure you are too modest, Miss Portman."

That earned him an almost scathing look. "No, I am not. Perhaps nine years ago when I was still considered a young miss, but now I leave modesty to those to find it of value. I am perfectly frank, Mr. Alchurch, and perfectly honest in my frankness."

"There is great value in that as well," Mr. Alchurch insisted, completely unperturbed. "Lady Standhope is inclined to see good things in everyone, likely even where we cannot see it in ourselves. Perhaps she has found you good company and delightful thus far, even if you do not believe you are generally considered to be so."

Miss Portman now surveyed him through narrowed eyes. "You are naturally good-natured, aren't you, Mr. Alchurch?"

Webb laughed at the almost disappointed tone of her voice, but also the accuracy of her assessment.

"I am," Alchurch admitted. "I'll not deny it."

"Which serves him well," Webb pointed out. "Mr. Alchurch is the curate at the parsonage at Goulding."

Miss Portman wrinkled up her nose as she looked at Alchurch again. "With your surname, sir, you willingly pursued the church?"

Webb had to bite down on his lips hard to keep from snorting with laughter now. He had wondered the very same thing from the day he had met Alchurch, but hadn't found the nerve to ask the man straight out. How many other parishioners had felt the same? And within two minutes of being introduced, Miss Portman was asking it.

Alchurch was laughing himself. "You would think it rather on the nose, but I'm a third son and the only one in holy orders."

"One shudders to ask what your older brothers do," Miss Portman murmured, her eyes widening.

Alchurch leaned forward as though to impart a great secret. "The oldest is a baronet in Norfolk, and the next a captain in His Majesty's Navy. Suffice it to say, being only a curate is far too humble for them. My sister, however, is hoping I will perform her marriage ceremony."

Miss Portman cocked her head slightly. "And when is the marriage to be?"

"She hasn't said," Alchurch admitted, his smile turning crooked. "I don't believe she has received a proposal she is interested in accepting as yet."

"Well, one cannot fault her for thinking ahead." Miss Portman finally smiled, even if it was slight. "As my own sisters assure me, the devil is in the details."

Alchurch chuckled and saw something that caught his eye in the distance. "If you will both excuse me, I see Mrs. Jessop, and I must ask after her son. He injured his leg the other day, and she was greatly distressed." He bowed and left them, his face already a mask of concern.

Webb raised a brow as he departed, watching him for just a moment.

"Did he just...?" Miss Portman asked, not finishing the sentence.

"He did," Webb confirmed on a sigh, turning back to her. "He is, quite unfortunately, exactly the sort of man one hopes a man of the church should be. I have never met a less hypocritical person in my life."

Miss Portman shook her head slowly. "I'd inquire as to the veracity of his claims on Mrs. Jessop's son purely to ensure it was not my conversation that sent him running, but I can see their conversation from here." She looked up at Webb, her mouth curving slightly. "Refreshing to have a gentleman not entirely obsessed with flattery or social pressures."

"Has that been your experience?" He made a face of

31

consideration, nodding in thought. "I suppose that would be rather frustrating to endure time and again. And yet, I can see the efficiency of doing so, from their point of view. There is a task to be done, and for most of them, better to have it done quickly and return to a life without that hanging over one's head."

"You seem to be removing yourself from the activity," Miss Portman mentioned with a sort of detached air, though her eyes were quite fixed. "I consider myself removed due to my age and unpleasant nature. What is your excuse?"

A trifle startled, Webb replayed his own words back in his mind, then found himself grinning as he realized he had done just that. "Habit, I suppose. I…well, I am a widower. Eighteen months now, and I am not used to socializing without a wife to claim."

Miss Portman's expression softened at once, making her appear several years younger, despite not looking in any way aged to begin with. "Forgive me, my lord, I did not realize…"

"How could you have?" he asked gently. "We've only just met. There is nothing to forgive."

She dipped her chin in a brief nod. "Thank you. And you have my condolences. Was it sudden?"

Webb gave that some thought, surprised that he did not feel the stabbing pain in the center of his chest with the same acuteness he was used to. "No, she had been ill for several weeks, so it was anticipated. But at the same time, it felt sudden to lose her. We had been childhood sweethearts, friends long before anything more, and I don't know that anyone is prepared for such a loss, no matter the conditions."

He hadn't meant to say so much, nor to speak with such intensity, but it had quite simply come tumbling out that way. As such, the silence after his speech was a trifle deafening, and all his internal organs seemed to wince at once.

"My lord, I think I need to back out of this conversation and find the hole I seem to be in," Miss Portman said after a moment, the tension now returned to her features.

A startled laugh escaped Webb. "What hole is that? I am unaware of your being in a hole. You should have cut me off, Miss Portman."

The corners of her lips tightened, which he took to be an encouraging response. "I have yet to be accused of silencing a man as he talked about his late wife, and I would hope my lack of politeness would not extend quite that far."

"Perhaps, but it is hardly good conversation at a house party." Webb grimaced dramatically as he glanced about the room. "I must be grateful no one else heard me, or I might find myself uninvited."

"Would that really be so dreadful?" Miss Portman shrugged without taking in any of the other guests. "Then you might return to your previous holiday plans and feel no pressure to say or do anything that conforms with any aims but your own."

She had a point, and he wouldn't pretend otherwise. "Unfortunately, I have promised my sister that I would be here, and she is not the sort to let me go back on such a promise."

Miss Portman grunted softly. "I have three sisters myself, so I understand that particular issue."

"Are any of your sisters here with you?" Webb asked her, noting Lady Standhope moving towards the dining room.

"Thankfully, no," Miss Portman quipped, batting her lashes while giving a false smile. "Anna wanted to come, as she especially loves parties. But I was the only one invited, and it really is for the best. The three of them are so cheery and well-mannered, I look like a troll by comparison."

Webb had to smile at that. "But do they leap upon beds?"

Her smile faded into something far more natural and very pleasing upon her features. "Do you know, I don't believe they do?"

"Then I think we can safely say that you are not a troll

among them." He nodded firmly just as Lady Standhope cleared her throat.

"Darling guests," she announced among the quieting murmur of voices. "Dinner is served." She took the arm of the Earl of Westwick, the highest-ranking man at the gathering, and started the procession in.

"Might I beg a seat beside you, my lord?" Miss Portman asked in a low voice. "I don't know a soul here, besides you, her ladyship, and Mr. Alchurch, and I would certainly seem like a troll beside the holy curate and the effervescent hostess."

Webb raised a brow at her. "But not by the absent-mouthed widower?"

Her quick smile seemed to almost express delight at his response. "That remains to be seen, but I can at least feel that I am not being judged, which is an improvement."

Offering her his arm, Webb managed a longsuffering sigh. "I may disappoint there, Miss Portman. I do judge from time to time, which is what keeps me going to church and listening to the sermons by good Mr. Alchurch. But I promise not to comment on any judgment of you to anyone here and keep those opinions to myself."

"Tell me your judgments, by all means," came the clear retort. "I deserve to know what they are, if I am the subject. How else am I meant to find the improvements I need to make?"

"Church," Webb insisted as they moved towards the dining room. "You will always find those areas there, and with Alchurch at the pulpit, you won't even feel guilt for having them."

"Church service without guilt," she mused. "That might almost make it worth going."

Webb snickered, trying to hide his amusement from anyone else. They entered the dining room and maneuvered around the massive table, perfectly set with festive décor, mountains of food, and more candles than Webb had ever seen on the same surface in his entire life.

Lady Standhope was clearly sparing no expense or effort for this house party, and he wondered if his house would be even half so festive when they brought the greenery in and set to work with the ribbons.

Then again, his brothers might get exceptionally creative with the décor and encourage his children to join them in their antics. Which would mean that he would have to pretend at loving the results so as not to hurt the feelings of his son and daughter, when it was really down to Fred and Bash for the eyesore. And then he would have to somehow hide the awful collection from the eyes of those who would pay visits during those few days or allow himself to become the brunt of mocking discussion in the village.

Webb paused near some open seats and pulled one out for Miss Portman, who sat easily and without any of the smiling gratitude some of the other ladies were employing for their companions. He took the seat beside her and surveyed the entire table as the rest of the guests took their seats as well. Many of them he recognized from social occasions before Mary's death, but some of them were strangers. He could only guess at their invitations from Lady Standhope, given the time of year and the risk of traveling in December, but then, he did not know how Miss Portman came to be invited either. Or how far she had come.

He'd have to find a way to ask her without being blatant. He was interested, but more out of curiosity than anything else. He wouldn't want her to mistake his interest for attraction, as she seemed the sort that would attack him directly if there were a misunderstanding, which might detract from the sort of warm party their hostess wished to hold. And considering the number of gathered individuals who knew him well enough to see him again, he would not enjoy being reminded of such a moment.

"Would you like to know anything about the gathered

masses?" Webb offered to Miss Portman in a low voice. "Many are familiar to me, and those that aren't, we could create information about them."

She pursed her lips slightly before they pulled into a sly smile. "I'll admit something to you, my lord: Creating information about people who are strangers to me is something I take great pleasure in. It saves me the trouble of judgment. Even if I am wrong, which I rarely am, I can never see them in their actual light again. It would be a travesty if I enjoyed social occasions, but as I do not, I find no harm in it."

Webb covered his mouth with a gloved hand, choking on laughs and trying to cough between them without appearing to take ill for anyone else. He leaned closer to Miss Portman, unable to keep from smiling at her. "If you are going to insist on keeping me laughing at inappropriate times, Miss Portman, I think we must be done with this 'my lord' business. If it will not scandalize you, call me Webb."

"Very little scandalizes me anymore," Miss Portman assured him as she removed her gloves and laid them in her lap. "If you are to be Webb, then I am to be Rose. And as for information, Webb, you might be able to make my task at this house party far simpler."

She matched his pose by leaning in, and murmured, "Tell me which of the gathered gentlemen are bachelors, and who might be persuaded to pretend at a love match with me."

CHAPTER 5

It was a credit to Webb that he had not reared back in shock when Rose had told him of her task. His face did show mild surprise, and as he pulled his gloves off, he cleared his throat.

"You are going to have to explain yourself a little more, Rose," he told her, his voice lower still than before, but ringing with the same amusement. "I did not have you down as a husband hunter, and now I am questioning my own instincts for creating information."

Rose rolled her eyes and wished the footmen had already filled her glass with Madeira. "It is very simple. My great-aunt, who is dying, secured my invitation to this house party. Surely you know me well enough from just the last few hours to suspect that I would never have come of my own volition."

His nod was very polite, which also did him credit, as did his honesty in doing so and not arguing her statement.

"Well," Rose went on, plastering a false smile on her face for the benefit of others, "she did so with the promise that if I found myself a husband of love and affection here, she would gift me a cottage in the Cotswolds and a stipend to maintain it. She knows I have only ever wanted a life away from Society and to do as I pleased, and even tempted me further by claiming it has a bountiful library."

Webb did her the courtesy of looking impressed as footmen began dishing out portions of the meal for them.

"I need not tell you that at my age, I have no expectations of making anything resembling a love match or even a comfortable one." Rose took a moment as her glass was filled before resuming. "And nor do I particularly care about that. But if I do this, I will not have to wait until I am five-and-thirty for my independence."

"What happens at five-and-thirty?" Webb inquired with a quick smile, appearing rather invested in the story for someone who had only just met her.

Rose snorted softly. "That is your first question?"

He shrugged his broad shoulders, his smile somehow more attractive for the air of laughter in it. "My first question was going to be your age, but then you mentioned independence at five-and-thirty, and now my curiosity will not be sated."

"Fair enough." She nodded at the footman's offer of boiled potatoes. "At five-and-thirty, if I am unmarried, my father will grant me the full amount of my dowry to do as I wish. I planned on securing a cottage for myself, somewhere away from London but close enough to my family that I might visit when I feel the desire. So, if my aunt's bargain allows me to have the same thing without waiting the additional years, why should I not try for it?"

Webb bobbed his head in a series of thoughtful nods. "Very pragmatic of you. How many years would you be waiting, exactly?"

Rose tried not to hold her breath, but the mention of her age was something that never failed to alter the way she was seen, if not the expression on the inquirer's face. And no matter how she pretended not to care about several things in her life as they were now, there somehow managed to still be a stinging sensation with those alterations.

"Six years from now," she admitted as clearly and concisely as she knew how while still keeping her voice low.

Webb's eyes narrowed. "Even more of a temptation, then. Six years is a long wait, regardless of the prospect. How much dowry is it?"

Rose felt herself slowly blink as she stared at this man beside her, unsure what title, exactly, he held, but fairly certain none of the peerage members inquired regularly about the financial prospects of a lady in Society. Particularly not to the lady in question.

"You're being very impertinent," she pointed out, feeling the need to give him the chance to adjust the topic of conversation or extend an apology if he were feeling in any way embarrassed.

"This from you?" he returned without spite, his brow quirking again. "Apologies if the financial notion is more offensive than your age. I am simply trying to get the appropriate scope of your situation. Marriage seems a steep price for someone uninterested in the state."

Now it was Rose who was on the back foot, and she looked away, considering what he had said with a fair bit of introspection. Why should he not inquire? She had started the impertinence by asking him straightaway to help her find a potential husband.

Fair enough.

"Ten thousand pounds," she told him softly, reaching for her wine and sipping just a little.

Webb made a whistling sound without being so uncouth as to actually whistle at the table. "A fair amount, to be sure. I can see the attraction in taking his offer, but if you want something badly enough, an avenue to achieve it sooner is equally attractive." He turned in his seat, looking at her more directly as his plate continued to fill with food from the footmen, as yet untouched by him. "But why pretend at a love match? What does that give you?"

"That is the crux of Aunt Edith's scheme," Rose admitted with bitterness, sipping some more Madeira for good measure before setting it aside. "She insists on love or affection for the match, as, in her words, it would be 'more difficult' for me. She refuses to let me marry for convenience and get the cottage."

"Your own aunt says it will be difficult for you to make a love match?" Webb scoffed openly, his expression scornful and pitying. "Not sure I like this aunt of yours. Where is the belief in your good qualities?"

Rose felt a little fond of Webb for his defense, misplaced though it was. "She knows I have few. She also knows exactly the sort of personality I possess, and she believes that I am capable of 'a great love,' as she calls it, if I'll just try a little harder. I don't know how she expects my efforts to prove more fruitful in that regard in a two-week house party at Christmas when several years of enduring the Season in London have failed to do so, but there's always the six-year wait if I fail."

Webb's brows lowered, more in thought than in anger. "So you think arranging your own match, pretending at the love your aunt seeks for you to fool her, might accomplish your aims without the same trouble."

"I am not the only one she has asked this of," Rose retorted defensively, plucking up her cutlery with almost jerking movements. "Three of my cousins are also supposed to marry in the time frame, all for love, apparently. Not for the cottage, as that would put us all in competition, but she has promised each of us something we greatly desire. Her instincts are markedly accurate, I must say. I have underestimated her, it seems."

"I am not judging you," Webb assured her with a calming gesture of his hand, then turned to his own plate. "That was a clarifying statement, not a judgmental one. I think it's a decent plan, actually."

Now *that* she had not expected, and her knife skidded off her meat onto her plate with an almost deafening screech that made at least five people near her twitch.

"You do?" she all but bleated. "I thought it was rather stupid myself, but I had no other recourse."

Webb shook slightly beside her, and she prayed it was with laughter. "I do," he eventually said, his voice choked and restrained. He took a moment to cut into his goose and take a bite, chewing carefully.

"Having made a good match of love and affection myself," Webb went on after a swallow, "I can safely say that one cannot simply will it into being, regardless of the prospect. And I am entirely in favor of outsmarting an aunt who thinks you are difficult."

"She also called me prickly and particular," Rose offered, as though it were helpful.

Webb looked as though he would throw up his hands in exasperation. "The gall of this woman!"

Sensing she was being teased, but that there was some truth in his reaction as well, Rose let herself smile, finding it far easier to do than she had expected. There was almost no force in it, and she suddenly wanted to laugh. "You're making me feel rather less stupid for all of this."

"I don't think you're stupid at all. The cards you have been dealt as a woman don't allow for independence unless you are exceptionally wealthy or married, and if you are married, you're not really independent unless there is an arrangement with your husband, or you are a widow who has been well set up." He made a face before shaking his head. "None of those options are particularly pleasing, so I can understand seeking a love match on your behalf, as it might be the happiest marital arrangement, but if independence is what you seek above all, arranging matters yourself is the way to do it."

41

He made it sound so sensible, and there was a great deal of relief in that. She might actually have an ally in this, unlike Aunt Edith's rendition of an ally—Lady Standhope—who would never understand Rose's feelings.

But before Rose got her hopes up too far...

She picked up her napkin and covered her mouth, turning towards Webb. "If you aren't serious about helping me, Webb..."

"Oh, I am entirely serious when I say I'll help you." He nodded fervently, chewing a bit of potato quickly. "Between the pair of us, we'll find an unobjectionable candidate who will play along adequately, allow you independence, and make a comfortable enough spouse for someone who doesn't want one."

Rose felt herself grimacing. "I'm not *entirely* opposed to a spouse. I've simply...lost the hope that I'll actually get one that I want."

Webb glanced at her, seeming far less surprised than he had been before, but there was some quiet, calming understanding in his dark eyes. And he did her the courtesy of not looking in any way smug or amused.

"Which makes me sound more whimsical than I have ever been," Rose added in a rush as her face heated. "But I trust you know what I mean."

"I do." He took a long drink of his wine. "A length of time filled with disappointment makes it difficult to summon something as vulnerable as hope. Far easier to harden oneself and stop wishing entirely. It hurts less."

"Precisely," Rose whispered, lowering her eyes to her plate. "It's been so long that I barely remember what made me hurt, but I remember the hurt."

"I understand," Webb murmured.

How in the world had they come to this serious admission of difficult feelings? And how did Webb know exactly how she had felt? Exactly how she *did* feel? How she had become this version of herself? It had never felt far from the truth of who she was, and yet…

And yet she was not always so outspoken and harsh. That had come with time and with hardening.

Somehow, he knew that.

"I don't want a cold marriage," Rose insisted, finding some strength to her voice. "I just want a quiet independence, and a husband who won't mind that I do."

"Seems simple enough."

She found herself laughing at that. "Glad you think so, but I cannot pretend others will be so reasonable."

Webb smiled at her, or perhaps at her laugh. "Reason does not always follow where it ought, does it? But I have learned the value of reason as I have aged, and it has served me well."

"Congratulations." She tried to quirk a brow at him, just as he had done earlier, but she was quite sure she had only managed to make an ironic face, which would do well enough. She had managed to keep much cynicism out of her tone with that single word, but he could not escape her dry humor entirely.

Webb glanced to his right along the table, then turned and looked on Rose's left, twisting his mouth as he did so. "We'll have to do some investigation, Rose. I've been away from social situations for the last year and a half, so the nature of some of these bachelors has gone a bit hazy in my mind."

"That is quite all right. We have two weeks, after all. And I have no idea when my aunt will come and visit here, so our progress will simply have to be what it will be." She shrugged a little as she focused on her meal.

"Your aunt Edith is coming here?" Webb sputtered softly, shaking his head. "Whatever for?"

Rose was loving the manner in which Webb reacted to her story and situation. He was perfectly in line with her own feelings, and it only solidified, in her mind, that Aunt Edith's eccentricity was indeed that, and not some perceived state that only existed in Rose's mind.

"To check on my progress, of course. What else?" She grinned rather playfully. "Do you really think a woman who has set this entire scheme up for me would not be personally invested in how it plays out?" She rolled her eyes, sipping her Madeira.

Webb made a face as he chewed part of his meal. "Now I am even more determined to help you thwart her ladyship for your own happiness." He nodded once and began gesturing with his cutlery as he spoke. "You shall have exactly what you want and nothing less. I have a fiendish dislike for the machinations of people where they directly impact the lives of others."

Rose released a breath of surprise and amusement. "Where were you when I had my coming out? My mother was an almighty tyrant."

Chuckling, Webb speared a potato and popped it into his mouth. "I'm afraid even I have no power over the mamas during the Season. That one we will have to set aside. But in this? I think I can help you."

A sudden though struck Rose's mind with such force she needed to take a moment before speaking. "You're not about to suggest yourself, are you, Webb? Charming as our conversation has been and promising as our alliance seems, I would hate to think…"

He was laughing before she finished, and she trailed off, waiting. "No, Rose, I am not about to suggest myself. I've had a successful marriage already, one based on friendship that love blossomed from. I plan on finding the same again, if I can, because that is the sort of life I want to live and marriage I want to embrace. I see no reason why you cannot have the same freedom of choice in your life, no matter what your aunt or Society says, and I should like to see you have it. Nothing more, nothing less."

"So you are the great humanitarian who will assist me," Rose suggested wryly, relief that he was not toying with her for his own ends washing over her.

"Don't endow me with virtues I do not possess," Webb scolded, still half laughing. "By engaging in this form of mischief with you, I achieve my promised aims of returning to a social life without having to venture so far out of my current understanding of my own comfort. I will be able to tell my sister, hand on heart, that I was indeed engaging with others and participating fully in the events here."

Ah, now that made things a trifle clearer in Rose's mind, not to mention even more acceptable.

She began nodding in thoughtful approval. "Self-interest is always the more honest motivation when one is appearing to be a humanitarian. The scheming on your part is admirable, Webb. I commend you, and now I don't feel nearly so crass for asking for your assistance in my own."

Webb inclined his head in a playful nod and held out his glass of wine. "To our mutually beneficial mischief, then."

Rose tapped her glass to his, the pure tone of the contact ringing quite proudly out between them. She sipped quickly, then began snickering as she caught sight of others looking in their direction after the clinking. "We may have to contend with some mischief in gossip from the other guests. Speculation runs rampant in confined spaces, and we cannot hope to escape it. Look."

Webb followed the direction of her gaze and made her laugh even harder by toasting those who were blatantly staring at them. The guests averted their eyes, but Rose saw how their mouths moved, and presumed their continued conversation would be on the subject of Rose and Webb's unconventional relationship.

No one would know the full story, and speculation would

only help her cause, should word reach Lady Standhope of her having found confidence in an eligible male guest.

Surely, she and Webb could manage convincing acts instead. He seemed to have an eye for the company, and she hoped he also possessed a knack for understanding people. It was on his recommendations and observations she would act, so she had to trust him.

And pray that he really was as self-interested and noble as he'd made himself appear.

"We'd better talk of something else," Webb said as he returned his attention to his meal. "Possibly disagree on something. Otherwise certain mouths will run away with themselves. Tell me, what do you think of novels, Rose?"

CHAPTER 6

He hadn't expected to enjoy the first night at the house party, gracious hostess though Lady Standhope was, but he had to admit that Rose Portman was the most unexpected form of good company Webb could have hoped for.

Indeed, he had never met a cynic who was less sour about life and less biting in their commentary. She was rather frank, he would grant her that much, but she was never insulting in her honesty. He found her pessimism rather amusing, considering how she had leapt on her bed when he'd first seen her, and wondered what else she might do in private that would be at odds with the persona she presented.

Did she twirl around her rooms when putting on a new gown, as his daughter did? Did she ride astride and let her hair dance on the wind? Did she read novels aloud to herself and do voices for each character? The possibilities were endless, and he was half-tempted to secretly seek her out during the house party for more opportunities to catch her unawares.

Fascinating creature, and his curiosity was certainly piqued.

If he got nothing else from this experience, at least he'd found some entertainment.

He was struggling, however, with the concept of being on one's own for a good portion of the day, as they were now. Breakfasts had been available for three hours or so, and there had been a sort of cold luncheon as well, for those still about the house. Many of the gentlemen had gone out shooting, though Webb hadn't opted to join them.

The ladies were occupying themselves with their usual tasks for daylight hours, as far as he could tell. Drawing, reading, embroidery, and walking were just a few of the activities he'd witnessed as he wandered Fairview, and he wondered if anything of the sort was truly engaging for them. He had yet to find Rose as he'd gone about this aimless pursuit, so he could not ask such a question as yet. His sister would have told him just as frankly, were she present, but he'd never paid all that much attention to the occupation of ladies during the day, so it had never occurred to him to ask her.

As for himself, Webb would have much rather been home at Downing and going over the ledgers with his estate manager. With St. Stephen's Day approaching, he liked to have a more specific understanding of what his tenants and servants had done throughout the year and to be able to gift them generously but accordingly. He had no doubt Mr. Parker would arrange the details with perfect integrity and understanding for how Webb would handle matters, but the distance between himself and his duties was not something he was comfortable with. He could have ridden across his lands again while the children were at their lessons, could have looked ahead to the planting season for his lands and tenant farms, taken his children to the village to find small presents of gratitude for their servants...

But no. He was here, a guest in a neighbor's home, and utterly bored.

Eventually, his wandering led Webb to the Long Gallery on the first floor, and he smiled to himself as he strolled along it.

Kitty and Pierce would have torn around this space at top speeds, racing each other from end to end before creating some spectacular course full of twists and turns, winding this way and that, Kitty falling over at least twice as her haste got the best of her balance. They had a gallery at Downing, but it was nothing compared to this.

Most of Downing was nothing compared to this, actually. And he had always been quite pleased with his home. Not that he was presently feeling shame, as he knew that Downing was well set up and still boasted fair prospects and immaculate gardens as well as prosperous farms. It was still regarded as one of the finest estates in Yorkshire, but this place…

There was nothing to compare to Fairview, and that included royal residences he had seen.

"Well, well, well… Lord Downing in the gallery. What are the chances?"

The dryness in the voice made him smile, as did the now familiar tone. A feminine voice without trills, lilts, or breathiness, almost perfectly crisp and somehow filled with all of the wry notes that had ever been left unspoken in polite conversation. Warm without being inviting, and polite without being deferential.

It could only ever belong to Rose Portman.

She was coming towards him from the far end of the Long Gallery, the blue of her eyes standing out even more due to the almost purple shade of her gown. She had pushed the sleeves back to her elbows, and the sight made him want to grin. He was quite positive that her mother would have scolded her at one point for stretching out the fabric of the long sleeves in such a way, but he suspected there was no telling Rose what to do or not do, especially at this point in her life. She was beyond caring about what anyone thought but herself, and it was remarkably refreshing to find that in someone who had not become entirely bitter and in some way scandalous.

There was no scandal to Rose. Only a desire for liberty.

And she was a determined enough woman to claim it for herself, even if he did not assist.

He liked that about her. She was no damsel in distress, and he was certainly no gallant knight. She was marshalling her own troops and looking for allies in the battle ahead, and he, still trying to get his own lay of the land, only hoped to not be a hindrance.

"Miss Portman," Webb greeted with a half bow in her direction. "Is it so shocking that I should be in the gallery? Have I managed to destroy your perceptions of me already?"

She scoffed just loud enough for him to hear as she approached. "No, not really. I only meant that in the vast scope of this entire house, I managed to find you in one of the places I was already venturing."

Webb cocked a brow at her. "Were you trying to find me?"

"No, of course not." She snorted softly and turned to face the portrait he was standing nearby. "As I said, I was already coming here. Why are you not out on the hunt?"

"I didn't think a hunt necessary when we already have one on the agenda, and I don't really trust Mr. Fordham with a gun after the amount of drink he consumed last evening." He shrugged and squinted at the portrait before him. "Do you think the gentleman painted found this likeness flattering?"

Rose snickered and clasped her hands behind her back. "I shouldn't think so, but perhaps he was a pock-riddled sort in life. In which case, this would be a flattering likeness indeed."

"There's a thought I hadn't considered. One must always consider the pox in previous generations." He nodded thoughtfully and moved on to the next picture, Rose falling into step beside him. "What of you? Why are you not reading or drawing or whatever it is that ladies are expected to do during unscheduled time?"

"Because I am dreadful at drawing, for one," she replied simply, "and I wanted to see the house, for another. Exploring grand houses is an underrated experience and would be one of my favorite pastimes if it were allowed."

"Is it not allowed?" Webb asked with a curious look, trying not to smile. "Are we flouting the laws of convention at the moment?"

He felt a surge of pride and satisfaction at the dramatic eye-rolling that Rose bestowed on him. "No, of course we aren't. I only meant that one cannot constantly be wandering grand houses. We all do it, but how often do we talk about it? According to my mother, it is a great mark of brashness to be always applying to housekeepers to see inside estate houses. Yet it does not stop her from asking our innkeeper to engage in such application on her behalf when touring the Cotswolds every other year. She wants to see all the great houses in the land, but she'll never admit it."

"That sounds like a problem very specific to your mother," Webb suggested with a hint of laughter. "Why deny our innate curiosity of such places? It does nothing for us, and manages to hem us in, so to speak. Tell your mother that if she ever comes to Yorkshire, she is more than welcome to tour Downing House."

"I will tell her no such thing," Rose retorted at once, surprising him with her vehemence. "You've done nothing to earn the misfortune of her presence in the privacy of your home. I love her, of course; she is my mama. But really, Webb, your politeness must have its limits. For your own sake."

He had to laugh at that, his mind venturing to thoughts of his own mother, who was due to arrive at Downing from the dower house today. She'd be focused on entertaining the children while she was in residence rather than on anything particularly festive. In her mind, the Christmas holidays were more a time of reflection than celebration, and that somber note had been her attitude towards all holidays since Webb's father had passed away ten years ago. She was not opposed to celebrations, nor would she be a depressing influence on any such occasions, but one would notice the strain in her features the longer she attempted enthusiasm.

But before all of that, she had been fairly exuberant in all things, especially under the influence of his father, as far as Webb could recall.

"I'll simply plan to be away at the time," he told Rose with a nonplussed smile. "She can meet my mother and the two of them can judge my house to their hearts' content without my being aware of any of it."

Rose's brows rose, accompanied by a dubious expression. "Would your mother not tell you her thoughts afterwards? Or now, rather? Surely she sees your house on enough occasions to express her opinions."

"Oh no. Quite the contrary." Webb shook his head very firmly, examining but not really taking in the landscape panting before him. "My mother never expresses her opinions—vocally, at any rate. One must decipher her facial expressions to get an idea, but even then, there are no explanations."

"Well, that is entirely unfair," Rose insisted, her face wreathed in understanding and sympathy. "How can you possibly know what she particularly objects to and what she would prefer if all you can tell is that she is unimpressed?"

"We have all asked that question our entire lives," Webb assured her. "She was vocal enough when she was interfering in my life, and I am certain she still is with my unmarried brothers, but no longer with me. She visits my home from time to time, but she loves the solitude of her dower house more and more as time goes on. I've had to resort to my children writing her letters begging her to visit for her to make the journey across the grounds."

Rose tsked a little, shaking her head. "I'd offer up one or two of my sisters for your brothers as recompense for your efforts here, but alas, they are all married. And it would be a bit like living in a place where it is always warm and sunny, everything is agreeable, and nary a cloud will mar the sky."

Webb winced dramatically, more to play along than anything else. "What would England become without its customary rain? And to be constantly overheated? I've been to Spain, and it is a lovely visit, but not my preferred style of habitation."

"I quite agree, which is why I do not mind spending Christmas apart this year." She moved on to the next portrait, this one of an elderly woman with minimal wrinkles, dressed in excessive finery. "Now this is an unfair estimation of aging if ever I have seen one. Is it really such a crime to grow old?"

"I've never thought of getting old as a crime," Webb informed her, casually striding to view the portrait more closely. "But then, I am a man."

"Oh, indeed?" Rose gave him a questioning look, her eyes wide. "You should tell people that earlier in the conversation. It might save them a great deal of confusion."

Webb gave her a sardonic look, which earned him a teasing glance in response. He turned his attention back to the painting. "A man, particularly a gentleman, can grow dignified with age and is always a candidate for social occasions and aims, be they matrimony, fortune, or influence. A woman, on the other hand, is considered to be more and more insignificant with age, unless she is very wealthy, very titled, or very influential. I have met far too many ladies who become diminished versions of themselves as the years go by, and I have always thought it quite a shame."

"You know several old ladies?" Rose asked him dubiously. Of all the parts of his statement she chose to comment on, *that* was it?

Webb dropped his head, snorting softly with laughter. "Well, you know. Aunts. My mother. My mother-in-law. Neighbors. You get to know a few over the course of a lifetime."

"I suppose so. If we are still friends when I am old, Webb, do make sure that I am painted with wrinkles, will you?"

He glanced over at her, finding her even more fascinating now than she had been a few minutes ago. "Friends already, eh? Very well, Rose. I shall ensure that every single wrinkle is painted in exact detail and illuminated with the proper lighting for the artist."

Rose smiled at that, still staring at the portrait before them. "Thank you. I cannot promise to have wealth or titles, but I think I can work for influence. Though, to be fair, I have very little intention of being a fixture in London Society. I have never enjoyed it, and I doubt that will change whether I am married or not."

"That all depends on how you look at it, I suppose. A widow can find her entertainment and enjoyment wherever she likes, can she not?" Webb folded his arms, giving Rose a daring look.

She sputtered lightly and wandered to the next painting. "We haven't even found me a husband yet, and you've already killed him off. So are we looking for the perfect superficial husband who will leave me alone and we live happily ever after apart? Or are we looking for someone we can murder someday?"

Webb clicked his tongue a little as he considered either option. "I don't think we should opt for a life of crime so early in our efforts. If the husband we get for you doesn't become the husband you deserve, then we can revisit the idea. You could still be an influential older woman without being a widow. If you wanted."

Rose made a face, passing the next family portrait of a portly man with too many neck ruffles. "I'd rather be influential in my local society. There is nothing that says all influence belongs to London, nor that Society does. I shall enjoy being a free-spoken older woman, locally terrified and respected, secretly admired. Perhaps I will even host Christmas parties and let revelry commence within my discerning eye."

"Revelry?" Webb repeated, nodding in thought. "You'd permit revelry at your parties, Miss Portman?"

"Within reason," she assured him as she walked beside him. "One must allow the festivities to be festive, after all." She looked around the gallery, her eyes narrowed. "Do you think the tradition of decorating for Christmas on Christmas Eve might be a little outdated? Why couldn't we decorate earlier? As part of Advent, even. Is the risk of bad luck really so great that we cannot be festively adorned in our houses for longer?"

Webb tried to imagine the space with garlands and greenery and the like, and he could see it all, brightening up the gallery and reminding those wandering here of the time of year. A house this size would have endless amounts of work to be done for such decoration, and the servants surely could only have that task alone for Christmas Eve. Would it really be so bad for them to stretch that work out for a couple of days and have the place be bright and cheerful for a bit longer than a scant few days? And families around here seemed to enjoy helping with the decorating process, so it would not all fall on the groundskeeping staff or the footmen. Why shouldn't it extend longer and let the good spirits of the holidays make up for the risk of bad luck?

"I don't see why not," Webb murmured, now ignoring the paintings around them entirely. "But I have no doubt that Lady Standhope has her decorations already prepared and ready to be hung from the very first waking moments of Christmas Eve. At Downing House, we are far less prepared. Perhaps I might tempt you to escape the house party with me for a time and help us with our preparations. Tomorrow, if it suits."

Rose looked at him in surprise. "You're putting them up tomorrow?"

Webb hissed loudly. "No, I am not ready to tempt fate yet, but we'll do all of the work involved in preparing the decorations tomorrow so that they may be hung on Christmas Eve the following day. If you will not mind sharing some decorating time with an exuberant three-year-old girl with a penchant for ribbons and an accident prone four-year-old boy with his father's eye for detail—that is to say, none—then it might be a trifle enjoyable."

"If it is better than wandering around to fill time, then I should be delighted to come." Rose turned to him quickly, her eyes round. "Don't tell Lady Standhope that I am bored already. I love exploring her house, but it is so large that I have to do so in portions, or I risk getting lost. A change of scenery and company would be most welcome."

"Well, let me ask you this, on the subject of what ladies do for entertainment," Webb mused as they neared the end of the Long Gallery. "Do any of you actually enjoy drawing and embroidery and the like?"

Now Rose began to laugh, full-bodied and rich sounds, her head falling back and her throat practically bouncing with each ripple of laughter. "No! No, of course we don't! Embroidery is meant to occupy our fingers and our minds, and sometimes the skilled ones make work to be admired, but mostly it is a way to fill time. Those who enjoy art do enjoy drawing, but those of us forced to take hopeless drawing lessons dread having to continue pretending all of that. Some enjoy music, and I appreciate those who do, but again, I was not one. Walking and reading are the pastimes I enjoy best, given my lack of skills in other avenues. But our entertainment is not the focus of the activities we are expected to engage in."

"Then what is?" Webb asked, truly curious now.

Rose tossed her head and fluttered her lashes. "Our accomplishments, my lord. For no gentleman of status and fortune would dream of marrying a young lady who cannot properly embroider."

"Ah," he said with a sage nod. "I had forgotten. That was, of course, my chief requirement when I was looking for a wife."

"Very sensible. I am certain you were not disappointed." She grinned up at him, making something tug behind three of his ribs. "Do you know what Lady Standhope has planned for us this evening? It is not a ball yet, is it?"

Webb shook his head. "No, I believe there is no ball until Christmas Eve. Tonight is festive parlor games, so that we might become better acquainted."

"Well then," Rose told him, "we shall have the chance to sniff out some potential husbands tonight. My aunt would know very well that I would never fall in love with a dunce or a bore."

"I shall watch for those poor souls who fit such labels," Webb vowed with all due solemnity, fighting laughter, "and have them struck from our list."

"Marvelous." Rose sighed and turned to face the Long Gallery once more. "Shall we walk the other side now? We ought to pay our due diligence, after all."

Webb smiled down at her, suddenly finding himself entirely at his leisure and without any boredom in sight. "Indeed we ought, Miss Portman. Let us walk."

CHAPTER 7

P arlor games were the worst.

Of most things, not just of evening entertainment options.

The worst of just about everything Rose could think of at the moment.

With an intelligent gathering, they might have been tolerable, but in a room that was filled with idiots, as this particular room seemed to be, it was positively interminable.

Or, she considered, perhaps it was simply filled with people like herself who were not answering the riddles and charades because they did not want to take a turn as the person in front of everyone, being subjected to their inane guesses.

That would be her hope, at least. Surely the majority of people could not be this stupid…

The festive theme of the games did not help anything, but it did bring a touch of levity into the occasion, which was undoubtedly what Lady Standhope had wanted. The Christmas rebus puzzles were practically sacrilegious, and Christmas charades had such a variety of answers from the guests that it became abundantly clear that the majority were calling upon any and all Christmas traditions they knew.

Why else would someone suggest an answer of mistletoe for a riddle that had spoken of boar's head?

Mr. Alchurch was now up in front of the group, reading his riddle card carefully. Then he smiled and raised his eyes to the gathering. "My first is in harvest rarely known, nor would it welcome be. My next in country or in town, each miss delights to see. And when drear winter's dress is shown, in joyous play my whole is thrown."

Rose allowed herself to lean against the arm of the divan upon which she sat, sipping her mulled wine just a little. She had noted from her first sip that Lady Standhope had emphasized the wine more than the mulled in this case, and until she finished her glass, she could not get another drink of any kind without appearing impolite.

"Weeds," someone in the group suggested.

"An ample product," another hooted with laughter.

"Ralph," a woman scolded. "He said, 'Nor would it welcome be.' We would welcome an ample product in our harvest."

There was more laughter from among the group.

"Beaux!" one of the ladies cried out. "For the second part."

"Excellent suggestion, Miss Plunkett. Most excellent."

"What is thrown in winter?"

"I am sure I do not know."

"Snowball," Webb announced from his post against the wall. He had been staring out of the window for a decent portion of the event thus far, and Rose had certainly noticed his level of distraction. She had hoped to catch his eye during the more exasperating portions, but he had not seemed to be paying attention.

"Snowball?" someone repeated in confusion. "You will have to explain that one, Lord Downing."

"Gladly," Webb replied in a crisp tone, setting down his

glass. "In harvest, rarely and not welcome is snow. And whether in country or town, a young miss loves a ball. Snow and ball, the whole is thrown in winter. Snowball."

An entire chorus of "oh" emanated from the group and Webb looked to Mr. Alchurch for confirmation of the answer.

Alchurch nodded and clapped at Webb for his response. Then he gestured for Webb to come up to the front for his turn.

Rose wondered if he had intended to do that or if, like her, he was just tired of the stupidity of others and was trying to end the game quickly.

Whatever it was, she looked forward to helping him get everything moving on so something better could take its place.

Webb took the next riddle from the pile and cleared his throat. "My first is a tree which with cedars will vie. My second's the tenderest part of the eye. My whole is a fruit which to none will give place, for delicate flavor, and exquisite taste."

The entire room stared at him in silence, several faces hanging perfectly slack as their minds seemed to work backwards rather than forwards.

Rose, for one, had to hide laughter behind a hand and sip her mulled wine once more to keep up her façade.

Webb gave her a warning look, the corners of his mouth tight.

Caught.

"Well, fir, of course, would make the most sense for cedars," someone called out.

"Does anyone know the parts of the eye?" a middle-aged woman asked.

"The pupil, but what in heaven's name is a fir-pupil?"

Rose felt her entire body shaking with mirth and had to look down at her knees to keep from exploding or spilling her wine. Spilling would create more of a scene than anything else, and if anyone in her family learned that she had spilled her wine at a party, they would begin to call her Edith. Though, in this case, it was not inebriation that would cause the spill.

"Did not Shakespeare say something about an eye?"

"Shakespeare said a great many things about a great many things. I do not think we can make that general claim and find it useful."

"But what does fruit have to do with anything?"

"Apple! Shakespeare said it in *A Midsummer Night's Dream!* 'Flower of this purple dye, hit with Cupid's archery, sink in apple of his eye'!"

"Fir-apple?"

Rose immediately began coughing and sputtering to cover the snickering that would certainly have become snorting if left to its own devices.

"Ah! Pine!" Mr. Alchurch announced, nearly coming out of his seat. "It is not fir, but pine. Pine and apple! The whole is pineapple!"

Webb pointed at him, nodding and giving him a smile of pride. "Indeed, it is."

Applause scattered among the gathering. Lady Standhope rose and spread her hands out magnanimously, her smile rather benevolent for an evening of stupid games. "Shall we do another game now? What about 'I love my love' for a while?"

"Oh yes, Lady Standhope!" the pair of sisters cried in eerie unison.

She nodded in apparent delight at such a response. "But rather than say 'treated,' as it is Christmas, let us say 'gifted.' I gifted her with our item of choice, whatever the letter. Will that be too complicated?"

Complicated? It was the simplest change ever. What sort of mind would find such an adjustment complicated? It was not as though she changed the entire script to be festive...

Still, obedient nods bobbed around the group and several

people moved their chairs to form a sort of circle for the game. Rose, for one, stayed exactly where she was. If that would exclude her, so be it. But others sitting near her were remaining, so she supposed she would be included after all. Webb actually came and sat in the chair that was just to her right, groaning a little as he did so.

"Tired, my lord?" Rose asked in an undertone. "Was the exertion of your riddle truly so taxing?"

He scoffed a little, shaking his head. "Only the effort of keeping my face in a relatively pleasant expression instead of engaging in the sort of behavior that might offend. If we were playing this game with my family, there would be vicious repartee going on and quite a lot of insults."

"Now that sounds like a version of charades I need to play," Rose remarked with a quick grin. "Far more entertaining and the sort of stakes I prefer. Now, what are your thoughts on this one?"

"Simple enough to quick minds and those who pay attention," he admitted with a shrug. "It truly depends on the company for how quick a mind must be. I've been in parties where you could almost be certain that each person would have the letter A, and while I do not suspect this will be quite that bad, I do not believe we will accomplish the first half of the alphabet."

"I find that generous," Rose muttered, glancing about the room. "Fir-pupil, indeed. What nonsense."

"You are harsh this evening."

"I find a lack of intelligence most frustrating. I know it is not always something one has a choice over, but there is no quicker means of irritating me than being stupid." She exhaled slowly, closing her eyes and willing the annoyance to fade. "It does make me tyrannical, and for that I apologize."

"You don't have to apologize," Webb told her with a pat to her hand. "As far as I know, you have not offended anyone yet this evening. I will let you know if that changes."

Rose clicked her tongue and slapped his hand away just as the game began across the circle.

"I love my love with an A," started Mr. Alchurch, "because she is amiable. I hate her because she is angry. I took her to Alnwick, to the sign of the arrow. I gifted her with apples, and her name is Annabelle."

The woman at his left took a quick breath. "I love my love with a B because he is balanced. I hate him because he is bad. I took him to Brighton, to the sign of the box. I gifted him with brushes, and his name is Bartholomew."

So far so good, Rose thought with a frown of consideration. But time would tell how long the trend would go without forfeit.

They made it to E before someone faltered, and Miss Proffitt did not seem all that bothered with being eliminated.

Starting over, the gentleman next to her managed A perfectly, followed by a rather tepid B, a cautious C, and a dull version of D if she had ever heard one.

Webb had E, and Rose stared at him in bemusement as he started. "I love my love with an E," he said dryly, "because she is energetic. I hate her because she is eccentric. I took her to Eton, to the sign of the elm. I gifted her with emeralds, and her name is Emily."

Rose nodded in approval and cleared her throat as it became her turn. "I love my love with an F because he is fair. I hate him because he is frivolous. I took him to Fulton, to the sign of the fox. I gifted him with figs, and his name is Frank."

A few of the ladies squealed in delight at the game going so far, and eagerly watched for what happened with G.

"Fair?" Webb whispered to her as the attention left them. "Are you leaving hints for potential suitors in that, Rose?"

"Energetic and eccentric, Webb?" she shot back. "It is as though you've laid me out as a paragon of good and evil in one go."

"The letter E is not particularly flexible," he countered. "Maybe on the next time around..."

Rose rolled her eyes and watched the group struggle over the letter I, which was one of the easier ones, in her mind, and now they had to start over again. There was laughter to be had, and she found herself joining in at times, especially when they would get really far along, and someone would make a mistake. She took another turn on the letter H, which went well, especially after Webb had made them all laugh over G, and they watched with bated breath as those who had succeeded thus far made promising progress.

This was clearly a group of the smarter ones, and there was hope of making it all the way through the alphabet, though Lady Standhope had told them they could exclude X, Y, and Z from the requirements, much to their relief.

They were making it, Rose realized as the letters continued to proceed around towards Webb and herself again. If it meant that the group participation could end all the sooner, she would be delighted. There were plenty of men here who had passable intellect, she could now confirm, and those of such intellect who had made no ridiculous guesses during charades were now on her list.

"I love my love with a Q," Webb said with careful, emphatic words, "because she is quick. I hate her because she is quiet. I took her to Quinton, to the sign of the quail. I gifted her with quills, and her name is Queenie."

There were several exhales of relief from the group. Rose nodded to herself as attention came to her. "I love my love with an R because he is regal. I hate him because he is rude. I took him to Ramsgate, to the sign of the rat. I gifted him with rubies, and his name is Robert."

The group moved on in excitement, praying they could get W and end the game. To the relief of all, they made it, and Lady

Standhope applauded in delight.

"And now, my dears," she announced as she rose, "we will engage in one of my favorite traditions of the season: Snapdragon!"

Cheers rose from the group and chairs were again rearranged, this time to all encircle a table. There was no way the entire group could fit at once, so they would have to take turns participating, which was perfectly fine from Rose's perspective. Snapdragon was an amusing game, but it had never been one of her particular favorites. Singeing her fingers wasn't comfortable, and she wasn't quick enough to avoid it.

Her brothers-in-law had become quite competitive each Christmas over the game, and she could not remember which of them had won most recently, but it was always worth watching them get so aggressively invested and burning themselves.

A bowl was set on the table and immediately the brandy within was set aflame, causing a great "oh" to rise appreciatively from the guests. Several raisins were dropped into the flaming depths, and then Lady Standhope indicated that the gentleman sitting just in front of her ought to go first.

"Who's that?" Rose whispered to Webb.

"Mr. Garner," he replied. "I am going to do you a great favor and say no to the prospect of him."

"Why?" she asked with a bewildered look. "He was intelligent enough in the other games."

Webb shook his head very, very firmly. "He is utterly insufferable, and I like people in general, so it really does mean something that I do not care for him. For your sake, you cannot even pretend to love him, let alone marry him to satisfy Aunt Edith's demands."

Rose was content to let his opinion guide her, but she certainly hadn't expected that.

Mr. Garner sat forward, his eyes on the flames.

"And now, everyone, let us sing the song and see how he does!" Lady Standhope gushed, conducting the forthcoming music herself.

Here he comes with flaming bowl,
Don't he mean to take his toll,
Snip! Snap! Dragon!

Take care you don't take too much,
Be not greedy in your clutch,
Snip! Snap! Dragon!

With his blue and lapping tongue
Many of you will be stung,
Snip! Snap! Dragon!

For he snaps at all that comes
Snatching at his feast of plums,
Snip! Snap! Dragon!

But Old Christmas makes him come,
Though he looks so fee! fa! fum!
Snip! Snap! Dragon!

Don't 'ee fear him but be bold —
Out he goes his flames are cold,
Snip! Snap! Dragon!

Mr. Garner sat back in satisfaction, four raisins in front of him. The other guests clapped merrily, and Miss Proffitt sat forward next, biting her lip and creasing her brow deeply in anticipation.

The song commenced again, but the words were a trifle lost among Miss Proffitt's squeals of discomfort and anxiety. Her fingers never even came close to one of the raisins, and she was now sucking on her index finger and waving the next person forward.

Miss Babcock gave Mr. Garner a decent challenge, also managing four raisins. Mr. Harris got three, while Mrs. Lorde and Miss Dawes picked one apiece.

The next group had one person get five raisins, but the rest were either one raisin or none at all. It all became rather raucous by the time the third group was taking part, and Rose never felt the desire or need to join in. She could participate just as enthusiastically by cheering for the others and singing the song; there was no cause for her to stick her own fingers into the flaming brandy.

Webb did not appear particularly interested in joining in either. Indeed, he seemed to be a little distant and far away from everything around them.

"Are you well?" Rose asked him with a hint of a nudge during the next round of the song.

He nodded easily, his brow furrowed ever so slightly. "Well enough. Simply missing the occasion to play these games with those I love instead of those I am getting to know. It is… strange to be doing this without them."

Rose felt something crease in a portion of her heart at hearing this, and she wished there were something to say or do to help him. But she was actually relieved to be away from her family for this Christmas, to be able to experience the holiday however she pleased without consideration to anyone else, apart from her hostess. No being forced into traditions she found ridiculous and no particular occasions to dread.

Still, she was certain she would miss the children when it came to be Christmas morning and she was not there for their little presents. It must be even more compounded for a father to be apart from his children.

"We'll see them all tomorrow, will we not?" Rose asked in an even softer tone.

Webb nodded again, this time with a smile. "Indeed, we will."

"Then perhaps you can encourage a daylight game of snapdragon, if it would make you feel better." She shrugged, wondering if he would take the suggestion well.

He looked at her with widened eyes. "Are you mad? Trusting my brothers with flaming brandy in the presence of my children? We might as well set Downing House on fire room by room. Really, Rose, you do have the most extraordinary ideas…"

CHAPTER 8

It was peculiar how excited Webb was to return to Downing House when he had only been gone for two days. But excited he was, and he could not wait to scoop up his children and roar to life as some dreaded Christmas bear that they would run from. If they were engaged in decorating, he could drape ribbons over his ears as he trudged after the children as this bear, and if he could find a sprig of evergreen somewhere in the house that wasn't spoken for...

"Why do you look positively scheming when we have actually left the site of our schemes?"

Ah, right.

He'd almost forgotten about his travel companion.

He turned from the window to face Rose with a quick smile. "Just trying to decide how to greet my children. I was thinking of being a bear."

She seemed to consider that, jostling a little on her side of the carriage. "That is a classic, to be sure. Have you done that before?"

"I have," he admitted with a wince. "That is one of the reservations. But if I could manage to snag some of the festive décor items, I could be a Christmas bear, which might improve matters."

"Hmm," Rose hedged, craning her head from side to side. "I would do something completely unexpected. Have you ever considered a cow out to pasture? Completely ambivalent and slow to move?"

Webb snorted a loud laugh and covered his mouth. "Pierce would grow so frustrated by the lack of interaction and movement. Kitty would stamp her feet and demand that I do something. It would be utterly perfect."

Rose made a sort of bowing gesture, smiling rather smugly. "You're welcome. And then, of course, the cow could decide to lie down on top of the children's legs... Wait, how old are yours again?"

"Pierce is four," Webb told her, smiling at the image of his dark-haired, fair-eyed boy with a stubborn streak. "And Kitty is three."

"Perfect," Rose said firmly. "Lying on the legs and mooing contentedly would be most appropriate."

Webb cocked his head at her. "How would you know?"

Rose shrugged a little. "I am the favorite aunt of my nieces and nephews, of which there are seven at this point. I must confess, I do prefer the infant stage to actual childhood. Once they've a mind of their own and clarity of speech, everything becomes a little less fun and a little more challenging."

"I will have to take your word for it," Webb said simply, grinning out the window. "Pierce is still very innocent at four, but heaven knows, the mischief cannot be long in coming."

"My sisters seem to enjoy the child stage well enough," Rose went on, almost as though he didn't say anything. "And my mother certainly enjoys them being older. I think it might just be a personal preference. And likely varies with each child. What is Kitty like?"

Webb's smile turned soft. "Kitty has her mother's fair curls and my dark eyes. She is shy until it serves her not to be and seems to dance when she walks. She is destined to be smarter than her brother, but she also merrily follows him everywhere. She's not above getting dirty and, right now, her favorite word is pony."

Rose laughed at that, clapping her hands together once. "That is utterly perfect. She is going to be the trial of your life when she turns sixteen, Webb, so you had better recruit some help."

He groaned at the prospect, covering his eyes. "Perhaps my sister will take her on. Emily is destined to be the sort of stern Society mother everyone fears."

"Then she will be most useful, I am certain." Rose suddenly gasped and placed both hands on the window, staring out. "Is that Downing?"

Webb nodded with some pride as the house came into view, one of the fairer prospects of it from this road. "It is indeed. Not so grand as Fairview, I grant you, but I'm rather fond of it."

"Who could blame you for that?" Rose breathed, her words fogging up the window a touch. "It's a perfectly situated country house and has both grandeur and charm. And look at all of those windows!"

"Yes, we do rather enjoy the light." He grinned at her awestruck expression and the upturn to her lips even as she gawked. "Come now, Rose. This isn't all that grand."

Rose blinked at it, barely seeming to hear him. "Perhaps not, but it is one of the loveliest houses I have ever seen." Her eyes slid to him, their bright blue shade illuminated by the color of the sky just through the window. "And you know how unlikely I am to give a compliment."

He held her eyes, his grin remaining exactly where it was. On her.

71

"Yes," he told her in a low voice. "I am well aware. High praise indeed."

There was something soft in this moment between them, something that wasn't friendship or any shade of romance. It was a sort of contentment, something binding, in a way, and it released a tension in his chest that he'd forgotten had been living there. No breathlessness, no change in pulse, no haze floating about his head, or ringing in his ears.

He was quite simply... happy.

Not entertained this time, or enjoying himself in present company, but happy. In a deeper, more indescribable sense.

Happiness. When had he last found that when he wasn't holding his children in his arms?

She looked away first, but he wasn't far behind. Strangely, his face didn't heat at all, and there was no embarrassment. No shame. No guilt.

Interesting, that.

Rose continued to enjoy the prospect of Downing the entire drive up, and Webb continued to enjoy the view of Rose enjoying the view. Her eyes darted over various aspects of the house and grounds, and he wasn't particularly paying attention to what. He was more interested in seeing the changes in her face as she inspected and noticed the details of his home.

She liked what she saw, that much was evident, but what he wanted to know was *what* she liked and *how much* she liked it. He wanted to hear her tell him all of her real opinions with the frankness he had come to know and appreciate. He wanted to see his house through her eyes, not his own, which had seen this house from the moment he was born. It was nothing spectacular or grand or lovely in his mind, other than that it was home, and he very much wished at this moment that he were seeing what she saw.

Whatever she saw.

The carriage pulled around to the family entrance, for which he was grateful. He wasn't in the mood for a grand entrance that his family would mock him for, nor one that would draw attention to Rose being there. She was a visitor, yes, but this was no standard business that required the usual pleasantries and formalities. This was his friend and co-conspirator coming to see what his life was like and to insert a bit of festive frivolity into their day without the fuss of the house party being involved.

It did not follow standard protocol at all.

Nor did he want it to.

Webb stepped out of his coach and turned to offer a hand to Rose, who took it quickly, her eyes still on the house and completely ignoring him, which made him smile. She released his hand as soon as her feet were on solid ground and looked around the perfect square that was the courtyard. The doors to the kitchens, the larder, the pantry, and another entrance for servants were there, as well as the door to the connection room that the family used when they came and went on less formal occasions. It wasn't that picturesque of a courtyard, as the bit of green in the middle had been trampled by his children and staff so often, it was a miracle the color still remained.

But Rose looked as though she might suddenly twirl in the center of it all.

In fact...

"Are you planning on twirling?" Webb ventured, injecting a wry but playful note into his query.

Rose looked over her shoulder at him, her blue eyes almost flashing in the bright sunshine. "I might. Would that upset your perceptions, my lord?"

"Not at all. It would rather reaffirm them." He pointed out the windows all around them. "I cannot promise it would be unobserved by others, however. And their perceptions are ones I cannot speak to."

She followed his gesture, her eyes narrowing. "Hmm. One would not wish to give false impressions. I shall refrain for the time being." She snorted softly and turned to face him. "Whatever gave you the idea that I would twirl, Webb?"

He shrugged easily. "You are a girl who flings and flops. Why would you not also twirl?"

"I haven't been a girl for several years," she murmured, her eyes lowering as she shook her head a touch.

"Except for when you fling and flop," he said, leaning forward just a little, though he was a fair distance from her. "And, I suspect, when you twirl."

Her eyes darted back up to his, and her mouth curved in a crooked smile. "One does like to ward off age however one can. Those actions are surely better than engaging in the poor table manners of childhood."

"Most likely." Webb straightened and nudged his head towards the door to the connection room. "This way. We'll see which member of the family we come across first and how far the Christmas preparations have gotten."

He moved into the connection room, not doing much to lead Rose other than walk in his usual way, and he could hear her quick steps behind him. It was a short distance to the stairs that would lead them up to the family rooms, but he ventured around them instead, wondering if the decorations might be waiting for hanging in the low drawing room here on the ground floor.

The sound of giggles met his ears and Webb felt his entire body relax as a smile crossed his lips. There was nothing like being at home with his children, and the sounds of their delight would never fail to lift his heart and his spirit.

"That sounds promising," Rose mused as they walked.

Webb didn't answer, his steps filled with a trifle more haste. It had only been two days, and barely that, but it felt like longer somehow.

He poked his head around the door to the Low Drawing Room, and saw his sister on the floor with five children in various stages of the decorating process, his mother sitting in a chair nearby with gold ribbon in her lap.

"Who is giggling in here?" Webb demanded in a booming voice, making all of them jump. "We don't giggle in this house!"

"Papa!" Kitty and Pierce leapt to their feet and raced to him, throwing their arms around his neck as he entered the room. He scooped them up with a growl, kissing each on their cheeks and hugging them close.

"Uncle Webb!" cried Emily's daughter Molly as she got to her feet and ran to him, grabbing a leg.

"Uh-oh!" He groaned and pretended to stagger. "We might be in trouble."

Molly's brother Dominic took up the challenge and hurled his dense three-year-old body into his other leg.

Now Webb wobbled dramatically from side to side, acting unbalanced and weaving every step with the added weight of his niece and nephew. Emily was grinning at the act, and even Webb's mother was managing a genuine smile.

He looked at Emily's youngest, sitting so quietly beside her. Susan had always been the quietest of the children, though she was the exact likeness of her mother, and her two years of life had been constantly filled with Webb's attempts to make her smile, most of which had failed.

But not all.

"Susie Lou," he teased with a silly voice and pretended strain in each step. "Are you a monkey, too?"

Susan put a finger in her mouth, giving him a rare widemouthed smile as she leaned against Emily, her perfect curls flattening with the motion.

"Hmm?" Webb put a little bit of a musical quality into his voice, trying not to feel too triumphant about the grin he'd already earned.

Emily whispered something to Susan, and the little girl got up and walked very sedately towards Webb, put a hand on his knee, and pushed with the tiniest of efforts.

Still, Webb moaned and carefully tottered to the ground amid all five children, making sure to use excessive dramatics to accompany his descent. The children cheered when they'd downed him, and Emily clapped to celebrate their victory.

"Now that the beast has been slain," she said amidst their laughter, "perhaps we might continue with our decorations? We want everything to be beautiful when we hang it up tomorrow."

Webb pushed himself up to his elbows, smiling at his sister. "What are we doing first?"

Emily speared him with a look. "Try thirdly. Some of us have been working at this all morning."

"I wasn't here!" Webb protested with a laugh. He turned to Kitty, who was patting his cheek in an attempt to get his attention. "Yes, my love?"

"Come see dis, Papa," she insisted, pointing to the place where she had been sitting.

He nodded at once. "Of course."

Emily cleared her throat and he looked at her quickly. She flicked her eyes to the doorway, then back at him. Webb glanced over his shoulder and saw Rose standing there, looking amused but reserved.

Which must be awkward.

Right.

Webb quickly got to his feet. "Apologies, Rose. Bit of an idiot."

"I spy an understatement," Emily muttered, widening her eyes.

Ignoring her, Webb gestured to his mother. "Rose Portman, this is my mother, Lady Downing. My sister, Mrs. Fellowes, and her children, Molly, Dominic, and Susan. And my own little ones, Pierce and Kitty. Everyone, this is Miss Rose Portman."

His mother and Emily inclined their heads in greeting, while the children waved easily. Rose did them all the benefit of a prompt and perfect curtsey.

"Do you want to help me plait ribbons, Rose?" Molly asked brightly, her dimples on as much display as her golden hair. "I'm not very good, but Grandmama is helping me."

Webb could have kissed his niece for her perfect embodiment of spring sunshine at that moment.

"Plaiting is my specialty, Miss Molly," Rose told the girl with a sage nod, stepping around the bits of greenery, ribbons, and beads scattered along the floor.

Webb watched her go with a fond smile, which was, most unfortunately, caught by his sister, who gestured for him to come over to her. He obliged, but did so by taking the slow route in the direction of his mother, kissing her cheek quickly before going to sit on the floor beside Emily. Kitty started showing him her work, but it did not stop his sister from beginning her interrogation.

"Who is she?" Emily hissed through a warm smile.

"Rose Portman," he told her without any inflection. "Weren't you listening?"

Something sharp jabbed into his thigh, making him inch away. He suspected it was a pair of shears, and those could be deadly in Emily's hands.

"*Who* is she?" Emily demanded as she focused on weaving ribbon through evergreen boughs.

Webb exhaled shortly. "A guest of Lady Standhope's. We've become friends in our mutual attempts to find the party less insufferable."

Emily hissed very softly. "Is it really that bad?"

"No, but she has her aims and I have mine, and we both need help. So we've come together to make sure they can be accomplished more efficiently." He shrugged and took the bit of hellebore Kitty had handed him. "I just wanted someone to make the party less awkward for me."

"And Rose?"

Webb pressed his tongue to his teeth, unsure if he should admit anything that was not his own story. "She's looking for a suitor," he hedged.

"I could find her one."

He glared at his sister, then held out his fingers for Kitty to drape ribbons over. "We're friends, Emily. And Rose feels as restless cooped up in a house as I do, so I suggested she come with me this morning to find a little more entertainment than Fairview held for us today. That is all."

"You call her Rose," Emily pointed out with a shrug, her eyes taking on an impish light.

"And she calls me Webb," he shot back. "It's an alliance, Em. Nothing more."

"Marriages have been made as alliances."

He pinched her upper arm with a sharpness he hadn't applied since childhood.

"Ouch!" she shrieked, leaning away.

"What are you two doing?" their mother demanded with the sort of warning tone she reserved for their brothers.

"Nothing!" they replied as one.

She rolled her eyes heavenward and looked at Rose. "I don't care what anyone says, Miss Portman. Your children never grow up entirely."

Rose smiled just a little, her blue eyes darting to Webb with an understanding that made him grin. "I should hope not. Whatever would they do that for?"

And despite his words to his sister, Webb's stomach clenched, while his heart seemed to take a breath all its own.

CHAPTER 9

The perfect thing about spending a morning's work with young children was that their questions were very rarely focused on speculation or propriety and more centered around the activity they were engaged upon than anything else.

Rose had never been so severely interrogated on her ability to thread beads in her entire life.

Blessedly, Webb and his sister were getting just as many notes and questions on their skills, and the only adult to escape such things was their grandmother, who was, in their eyes, quite perfect.

As a decent grandmother ought to be.

But the real trouble came when Webb's brothers appeared on the scene, hellbent on mischief and disorderly conduct among the children. Ribbons became tucked in cravats, sprigs of fir were shoved into hair, and someone started chasing all of the children around with a very pointed piece of holly leaf. Shrieks of delight mingled with fear filled the space, and it seemed whatever decorations had been planned would need to be revisited another time for anything productive to occur.

Strange for two grown men to cause such havoc among

children, but Frederick and Sebastian Rixton were rather perfectly attuned to what would provoke laughter and energy in each of their nieces and nephews, and they were determined to get it.

Webb seemed to view his younger brothers with a mixture of irritation, amusement, and surrender, and they were just as keen on provoking him as the children. Less interested in the laughter and energy portion, but the provocation seemed the point.

It worked well.

And yet, there was real affection between them, and Webb's smashing Sebastian's head with a small pillow when the man least expected it proved that. The laughter that erupted from everyone in the room, young and old, was warm and filled with love.

Rose hadn't thought her family lacking in any way prior to this, but... They had never laughed like that together. Her extended family, certainly, given the number of them and the variety of personalities among them, but her immediate family...

Not that she or any of her sisters would have hit one another in the head with a pillow, no matter what silly things they'd done earlier in life. But they'd always been so focused on propriety in her home. On being agreeable and acceptable and presentable. She had warm parents and smiling sisters, but they were rarely silly.

The silliness here... Well, it was delightful and captivating, and a little bit addictive.

They'd all moved from the Low Drawing Room on the ground floor to one of the others on the next, and it was a much larger room with far more comfortable furnishings. Only some of the greenery had been brought up with them, and the younger children had given up on their projects in lieu of more entertaining relatives.

Rose, however, worked intently with Molly, Pierce, and their grandmother on a particularly well-embellished garland. Webb was trotting his daughter on his knees just across from her, and she would not pretend that it was not remarkably appealing to see him thus.

He hadn't even been that appealing on their first meeting, despite fulfilling the tall, dark, and handsome categories with perfection.

His children adored him, that much was clear. He was their whole world, no matter how they loved their grandmother, aunt, and uncles. Their father was their everything, and they were his everything.

A sharp prickling in her finger brought Rose to her present moment, and she frowned down at it, a small droplet of blood appearing on the tip. She popped it in her mouth very briefly, shaking her head. "Clumsy."

"Oh, who hasn't done that five or seven times in the course of a sitting in embroidery?" Emily replied with a wince from the other side of her mother.

"I haven't," Frederick offered from his slouching position beside Webb on the sofa. He'd made no effort to appear like a proper gentleman in Rose's presence, which was rather endearing, actually.

Emily huffed. "Bash, be a dear and thump the back of his head, please."

Sebastian took a bite of his biscuit and obeyed his sister, earning himself a swat from Frederick, and the two began taking swipes at each other.

Rose watched them for a moment, lowering her hand to her lap. "Is that normal behavior for brothers?"

"Depends on the brothers," Lady Downing told her without looking up from her work. "Mine never misbehaved, and Webb rarely does, but those two seem to have developed the temperament of rabid boars at times."

"You could have had us trained better, Mother," Frederick replied, sniffing once and taking a biscuit from the tray on Sebastian's side of the table.

Lady Downing shook her head, eyes widening. "One did try, but beatings did not seem particularly humane or genteel."

"Mama!" Emily snorted before dissolving into giggles.

Frederick and Sebastian laughed along with them before Sebastian decided to start chasing Dominic around the furniture at a pace that Dominic could match. Kitty, seeing the fun, climbed off Webb's knees to run with her cousin away from her uncle.

Rose shook her head as she continued to string red beads together in a long strand for the greenery. "I must say, Lady Downing, that I've never seen a family so active with each other. I've three sisters, all married and with children, and my brothers-in-law are excellent fathers, but the way you all interact with the children is something I have never seen before."

"That was my husband's influence, I believe," Lady Downing said with a hint of a smile. "He was all fun and games all the time, and it was impossible to raise the children with any other manner."

"Not all the time," Frederick protested loudly, rubbing the back of his head. "I have a history of bruises back here from his quick hand."

Webb snorted softly. "You wouldn't have had as many if you'd learned your lessons the first time."

Frederick gave his older brother a dark look. "Says the one who told me how to duck properly to avoid them because he was getting his own."

Rose chortled, covering her mouth quickly to stifle the sound, which seemed to make Webb and Frederick laugh as well.

"It was quite the experience for me, motherhood," Lady Downing said to Rose in an undertone as her sons continued to laugh and tease each other. "I was more properly raised, likely as you were, but Rupert was such a wonderful, engaging, and fun man that I found his ways perfectly irresistible. And my children seem to be well mannered enough for other people and for social occasions, so all was not lost with my sense of propriety in parenthood."

"I am inclined to agree," Rose assured her, eyeing all of the siblings with more than a touch of envy. "The bonds between them seem very strong."

Lady Downing finally looked up, watching her children with a fondness. "They do, don't they? The boys try me, and Emily gave me quite the time of it when it was time for her debut, but there is something beautiful between them that surpasses anything that irks them about each other. And were their father alive, I can assure you he would be on his hands and knees on the floor and chasing the grandchildren."

Emily laughed beside her and nodded repeatedly. "He would. I have many memories of climbing upon his back while he chased after the boys and pretending I was on a hunt."

Rose shook her head slowly. "I don't believe my father ever got on the ground with us." She looked at Lady Downing with wide eyes, her chest tightening with horror. "I have never felt unloved, please don't mistake me..."

"Of course not, Miss Portman," came the maternal reply, a soft hand going to her arm. "There are so many ways to parent children, and many ways to show love."

She was grateful to hear that from a woman whose family was rather exuberant in their expression of affection.

"When are we doing the yule log, Mother?" Frederick asked around a mouthful of biscuit.

Rose looked at him in surprise. "Yule log?"

Webb was also looking at his brother, though his expression was one of familiar contempt. "Why are you asking Mother? This is my home."

Frederick didn't even look at him and simply put a hand over his brother's face, pushing him away. "Mother?"

Lady Downing gave her middle son a longsuffering look. "If Webb has arranged it, or Emily, for that matter, then Christmas Eve, Fred. As always. And there will be no seasoning it with brandy this year."

Her son gave her a very aghast expression. "How was I supposed to know that amount would be so very incendiary? And Webb's eyebrow has grown back well enough. A little anointing of the log, now that I know how much *not* to use, would only bring good luck."

"God save us," Webb muttered, shaking his head.

"If that's how you want to bless the thing," Frederick allowed with a benevolent nod, as though Webb had only made a suggestion. "Any traditions for your family's Christmas, Miss Portman?"

Rose blinked at the question, her brain suddenly going vacant as she tried to recollect Christmas with her family. All she could think of were lengthy church sermons and feeling as though she'd break her teeth on coins tossed into the Christmas pudding. Her sisters hoping for dolls every year, and Rose simply hoping she would *not* get a doll. Stealing marzipan and gingerbread with her cousins from the kitchens.

Webb was giving her a confused look now, his head cocked slightly as though her hesitation was a cause for concern.

In a way, it was, but only for her.

Did she have Christmas traditions? Or was it simply a day they observed because everyone else was?

"Well," Rose began slowly, searching every corner of her mind for some answer, "I think that one of my aunts introduced a sort of mulled hot chocolate at some point. Not with wine, though. I believe there was a touch of whisky along with cinnamon and ginger and cloves. Perhaps a bit of orange as well. They never let us children drink it, obviously, and even now, it is rare that we get a taste of it. We are all still too young, I suppose, in their minds."

"Now that is a drink I'd like to have!" Sebastian called out from his place chasing the children.

"Large family gathering, is it?" Frederick asked, ignoring his brother and folding his hands over his midriff. "That's always nice. Unless they're a boring lot."

Rose smiled, feeling rather fond of Mr. Frederick Rixton for his finding a positive view of her poor attempt at tradition. "They are not. Well, a few might be as individuals, but as a family, we're quite a bunch. There's an uncle who always tries to get an aunt quite soused before the night is through so she will spill all the family secrets."

Frederick nodded. "Excellent use of time. I approve."

"I shall tell Uncle George forthwith," Rose quipped with a grin, going back to her work.

"Any regrets at missing it this year?" Frederick asked.

Emily huffed in irritation. "Fred! Stop interrogating her!"

"What?" he protested, flinging his hands out. "She's a new face and Webb isn't telling anything, so I have to ask questions!"

Rose found herself laughing hard. "Webb isn't telling anything because Webb doesn't know anything. We've only been friends for two days, and there's only so much one can talk about at a house party surrounded by others at a festive time of year. And last night's parlor games…" She rolled her eyes dramatically for effect. "I have never felt so surrounded by idiots in my life."

"There's the Rose I know," Webb said almost proudly, pointing at her and winking.

Frederick hooted with laughter, while Emily seemed to be looking between Webb and Rose with some frequency.

Rose wasn't going to allow for more of that, so she resumed

stringing her beads. "At any rate, the breath of fresh air that is Downing House is most welcome."

"We've got you stringing beads and plaiting ribbons," Sebastian countered as he finally scooped Dominic and Kitty up, one under each arm. "Some fresh air."

"It would certainly be more fresh if you were of some help," Emily snapped with impatience that Rose sensed was mostly forced.

He hefted the giggling children meaningfully. "What do you call entertaining the children? Your husband is absent, I noticed."

"Not absent," a new voice corrected. "Occupied." A rather average-looking man with a round face and broad smile entered, every inch the country squire in dress, giving Sebastian a challenging look.

Sebastian shrugged, heaving the children as he did so. "Apologies, Bertram. Anything amusing?"

"Settling details of the hunt for us in a few days and sending out invitations to a few local families, not that you care about details." He came over to Emily and leaned down to kiss her cheek, his fair but thinning hair catching enough of the sunlight to tell Rose exactly where Molly got the shade of her hair from.

"I love a hunt," Frederick said on a sigh, still slouching on the sofa. "You going to come with us, Rose? Watch us go out and see which of us is the best Rixton?"

Bertram cleared his throat. "I already know the answer to that." He nudged his head towards his wife, earning him a fond patting on the arm.

Frederick gave him a doleful look. "Boo, Bertram. Bad form."

"Em doesn't hunt," Sebastian pointed out as he tossed Kitty onto the sofa beside Frederick and Dominic onto the sofa opposite, both children squealing in delight. "Therefore, disqualified."

"And Webb cannot use the title as his excuse," Frederick pointed out, jabbing a finger into Webb's side as he scooped Kitty onto his lap with his free arm.

Webb looked at him in disbelief. "Did you hear me say anything about any bleeding title?"

"Language, my lord," Sebastian scolded, miming a swat to the back of Webb's head from across the room. "There are ladies present you are not related to."

Webb looked as though he would throttle Sebastian if only he had the energy. "Stuff it, Bash."

"My apologies, Miss Portman," Sebastian said as he turned to her and bowed deeply. "My brothers are such brutes. Please, try to scrub all you have heard from your delicate ears."

Rose favored the man with the most superior look she could manage, smiling in the way her mother always said was too smug. "You're a bleeding blowhard, Sebastian Rixton, and if you weren't half so charming while you were, other people would say so."

Frederick and Webb laughed so hard they began to wheeze, but then they rose to their feet and applauded her. "Brava! Brava!"

Emily, on the other hand, had fallen onto the floor in giggles. Lady Downing beamed as she continued her focused work on the garland and ribbons.

"I like Miss Portman," Bertram announced to the entire room as Frederick and Webb resumed their seats. "What a refreshing guest."

Still laughing, Webb shook his head, eyes on Rose, making her cheeks heat, for some odd reason. "Isn't she just?"

Rose's throat tightened and she shifted in her seat, looking to Molly on the floor beside her. "What do you think, Molly? Is this string long enough?"

CHAPTER 10

There had never been a more favored guest at Downing House in Webb's memory, and he wasn't sure what to make of it. He was delighted, of course, that Rose had been such a favorite with his siblings, his mother, and his children, but he hadn't exactly planned on inviting her back during the house party when he'd brought her. He hadn't thought that far ahead, so how could he have done?

Yet now, she had been invited to Christmas Eve festivities, the Christmas Day feast, the hunt on St. Stephen's Day, and to try some of Cook's eggnog on New Year's Day.

Webb hadn't even extended those invitations to her. His family had.

Thankfully, Rose had demurred for the time being, as she was a guest of Lady Standhope and needed to consult her schedule before making any additional plans, which would give Webb plenty of time to gather his thoughts.

There was a ball that night at the local assembly rooms that Lady Standhope was insistent everyone attend. The villages in and around York celebrated Christmas and its season with great enthusiasm, if not fanfare, and nearly every night from the second

Sunday of Advent through Twelfth Night had some sort of party or concert. Due to their stay at Fairview, the guests weren't participating in all of them, but Webb was delighted that they would experience a few things in the village.

Especially if Rose could experience them.

It was becoming clearer and clearer to him that Rose was hungry for experiences in life other than what she had known, and he wanted desperately to give them to her, if he could. Her reaction to his family was a clear enough indication of that. Not in the least bit shocked, but entirely entertained and welcoming of every single one of their antics.

She was destined for more of them, as it happened, as they would be seeing his siblings shortly at the assembly rooms for the ball. It would give his brothers a chance to entertain her, if not interrogate her, and Emily would certainly ask a number of questions to sate her curiosity, which would then be reported back to their mother in short order.

The speculation about his relationship with Rose would run rampant among his siblings for the entire Christmas holidays, but he didn't mind. He would explain the details when this was all over and Rose was happily married off, having attained her cottage and stipend. She would have helped him to return to the world of the living and social present, which would satisfy his mother and sister.

He was simply having fun with Rose and enjoying her company, as well as her view of the world.

Tonight, he would have to get to work in helping her find suitable suitors. She could not exactly come directly out and propose matrimony to them, but she could get to know them in ways that might tell her if they would suit her needs. And then they could begin a decent pursuit of the gentleman and meet Aunt Edith's requirements.

Webb had always enjoyed dancing before Mary died, and

he hadn't danced at all since her death. To that end, he was not entirely certain if he actually enjoyed dancing or if he had simply enjoyed dancing with Mary. Tonight would tell him one way or the other, and then he could adjust his actions and activities accordingly.

Surely he could find enjoyment in a Christmas ball even if dancing turned out to not be enjoyable. He was determined to embrace whatever he could about Christmas this year and not think about the losses that had impacted the holidays of years' past.

But now he was waiting for Rose to come down from her rooms, having arranged for her, among two other guests, to come in his coach to the village. It was quite the feat to finagle getting Rose in his coach without looking as though he was scheming to get Rose in his coach. The other two guests were elderly women, so they would be excellent chaperones for those who might have been concerned about such things.

Then again, this was the countryside and not London. Chaperones were more advised than required, and no one batted an eye if they were not present.

"What the devil are you pacing for, Webb? Needing some exercise, are you?"

Webb snorted softly and turned to look down the corridor, his laughter dying in his throat.

Rose looked as lovely as he had ever seen any woman look, but somehow more. Her gown was not elaborate or even perfectly fitting, but it was positively ethereal on her trim frame. White with shimmering gold plaits and elements, white rosettes along the neckline and somehow scattered along her dark hair as well. Ringlets hung along her cheeks and ears, and the white ribbon in her hair appeared like a crown of sorts. Or a halo.

An angel, then. Rose was a beautiful, frank, secretly silly angel, and he needed to find his mouth one of these next moments or she was going to think he had lost his senses.

He would think he'd lost his senses in a few moments, too.

"Not at all," he all but sputtered, racking his brain to recall the teasing question she had asked him. "Only eager for the ball, of course. Aren't you?"

Rose raised a brow, making her bright blue eyes shimmer remarkably. "Thrilled. All Society girls long for a ball. Wasn't that the riddle made the other night?"

"You assured me that you hadn't been a girl for some time," Webb pointed out, elated that his wit and tongue had found their places again.

"Lord Downing!" an elderly voice he didn't recognize chirped. "Do not tell me you were making a commentary on Miss Portman's age!"

He looked behind Rose and saw two older ladies, both wrapped in shades of green and warm cloaks, heading towards them. Both were also giving him a rather severe look.

He wasn't certain which had spoken, so he addressed them both. "Ladies. No, I am not making a commentary. Merely reminding Miss Portman of her own words."

"Still not a wise decision," the lady on the left murmured, her many beaded necklaces jangling with every clank of her walking stick against the floor. "And Miss Portman is dreadfully young, is she not?"

Rose smiled at the approaching women. "I am nine and twenty, Mrs. Richards."

"A child," the other woman puffed pompously, her perfectly rouged cheeks matching the red coloring of the top of her walking stick. "Still in her bloom."

"Lady Clarke," Rose said scoldingly as she adjusted her gloves and lifted her cloak from over her arm. "I have it on very good authority that I am past my bloom."

Lady Clarke waved her walking stick a bit dangerously.

"The only ones who say that are the ones who regret the loss of theirs. You are blooming delightfully still, Miss Portman, and Lord Downing would agree."

All of the women looked at him for confirmation.

He knew his duty.

"I would indeed," Webb obediently replied, giving Rose a gallant bow. "Blooming radiantly."

"Well spotted," Mrs. Richards cackled. "Now, Lord Downing, will you take us to your carriage? I do not like to miss the reels at these balls."

Webb took the woman's arm and offered the other to Lady Clarke. She took it, then looked at Rose quickly. "Come take my arm, girl. Lord Downing doesn't have a third to spare and we must make him look like a gentleman somehow."

Rose coughed a laugh as she fastened her half cape about her. "I don't mind walking behind, my lady. I do it all the time with my family."

"Pah!" Lady Clarke sniffed loudly. "Being at the end of the procession and alone due to marital status is not the same thing. Come here and take my arm, I said!"

Rose gave Webb an exasperated look of amusement, but did as she was told.

There was a warm sense of unity and understanding that passed between them then, and the fact that Webb knew exactly what Rose was thinking without speaking and solely based on expression was oddly satisfying.

But really, what was he doing that for? Their companions were eccentric, and surely anyone would have reacted in a similar way to Rose and Webb. The understanding ought to have been present for strangers, let alone recent friends. He shouldn't feel satisfied or proud or smug or anything at all apart from allied in amusement.

Stupid. He needed to figure out what he had done with his

head as well as his senses because it was becoming more and more clear that they weren't present at all.

The four of them loaded up into his coach and were quickly pulling away from Fairview. Lady Clarke was on his right, while Mrs. Richards sat beside Rose, and conversation was immediately struck up. Mrs. Richards lit into an animated description of the guests she had gotten to know already, and whether she could see any matches being made among them. Webb wondered if she somehow knew about Rose's scheme for a match, until Lady Clarke jumped into the discussion with her own views, and the two of them were basically ignoring Rose and Webb altogether.

Webb saw Rose's fingers fluttering in a sort of wave and he looked up at her face, tilting his head.

Her eyes were wide, and she shook her head very slightly, flicking her gaze from Lady Clarke to Mrs. Richards, then back at him. Again, she shook her head.

Ah, she was afraid he was going to inform these ladies about her situation, was she?

He smiled very slightly and bobbed his chin in a brief nod, keeping his eyes locked on hers. He did his best to cast the words *do not worry* across the space between them, purely through his eyes and expression. He wasn't sure it would work, but there was only so much reassurance one could put into one's expression before it became a smirk.

And he did not want to draw the attention of their companions by his facial expressions, nor his focus.

They would notice every little thing the moment their attention was diverted from their matchmaking discussions.

Rose smiled back at him, her shoulders sagging. He would take that as relief, and there was more delight and satisfaction in seeing that than anything else. There was more warmth in the way she looked at him, in her gratitude, in her blossoming trust, than he had felt in anything away from his family in years.

He liked being trusted, he realized. And being useful. He liked knowing that someone knew they could rely on him for help and to keep their confidences. He liked being able to do something for someone else. He liked being a gentleman in deed as well as in status and word.

And he liked, very much, that it was in Rose whom he was presently finding this usefulness, trust, and confidence.

The assembly rooms were only a few miles from Fairview, and even from the street, any passerby could see that they were fully lit with candles. In fact, they were lit in such excess that any other light in the village was weak and dim by comparison. And as the assembly rooms were not a residence, there was a long-held belief that it was exempt from the curses attributed to early decorating for the Christmas season. Upon entrance to the rooms, Webb observed hellebore, holly, hawthorn, rosemary, ivy, and evergreen boughs and garlands decorating every single corner, tabletop, window, and open surface. Ribbons and red beaded strings wove throughout everything, and there were very specifically placed balls of mistletoe in doorways and over the occasional window.

York celebrated Christmas in a way that no other place did, from what Webb had seen, and after a few occasions of celebrating it in other places throughout his life, he had vowed never to do so again. He could not look around this room without feeling his spirits brightening at once. They hadn't even been particularly low, and yet they were lifting.

He adored Christmas, he reminded himself. He might have forgotten last year with the loss of Mary dimming every single moment of every single day, no matter how bright it might have been to others. But Christmas was always a much-loved time for him, and it was lovely to be reminded of that fact.

"Will I have the pleasure of dancing with you ladies this evening?" Webb asked of the ladies on his arms.

Lady Clarke rapped him on the arm sharply. "Naughty man, there is no way my joints will allow for such activity. And Anne-Marie's bones are even more frail."

"Speak for yourself, Louise," her friend snapped with a laugh. "I may try it before the evening is out." She looked up at Webb with a wry smile. "I do insist you dance with several ladies, Lord Downing. I know you are a widower, and quite the catch, but dance with several ladies and give them a lovely present for Christmas. I will say nothing of matches where you are concerned, only that you deserve a bit of fun."

Webb looked down at her with a fond but cautious smile. "How do you know my story, Mrs. Richards?"

She winked up at him. "Lady Standhope will have her favorites, my dear. Never fear, she has no schemes for you either."

"That is a relief," he assured her, catching Rose's muffled grin out of the corner of his eye. "I despair of schemes. Never engage in them myself, do you?"

Lady Clarke was now the one who chortled and released his arm to sit in a chair by a particularly well-adorned window. "Anne-Marie and I are the very epitome of matchmaking mamas, Lord Downing. We matched our niece and nephew without them being any the wiser, and they are so delightfully wed now that we're settled on making more perfect matches we have an eye for."

Oh heavens, it was worse than he'd thought!

Still, if they were certain he was not in their schemes...

"Do let me know how I can help, ladies," he said in a conspiratorial manner. "I'll even offer my house for your secret meetings if you can manage good marriages for either of my brothers."

The ladies looked positively delighted at this offer. "Point them out to us, my lord, and we shall see what can be done!"

Webb bowed, leaving them both to their seats, and turned to walk about the room, Rose staying by his side without looking as though she was accompanying him. "I cannot believe you would do that," she hissed between giggles.

"Turn my brothers over to matchmaking monsters?" Webb snorted without reservation. "I'll even write up biographies for them, if it helps. No shame with Fred and Bash, Rose, and it would only serve them right to deal with those two."

"The ladies or your brothers?" Rose inquired through narrowed eyes.

Webb shrugged. "Either. Both. They all deserve each other." He looked over at the dancing, already underway, filled with joyous whoops and hollers. "Fancy a dance or two with me tonight, Rose? You'll need a break from those you're pursuing."

She groaned a little, making a face. "I will, won't I? Very well, a dance or two at your discretion. If I seem like I may do something rash or imprudent, do come and save me. Whom should I dance with first?"

Taking all details into consideration, Webb looked around the assembly rooms in thought. "Start with Mr. Foyle, if he asks you. Or if you can convince him to it."

"A lady can always finagle an invitation to dance, my lord," Rose assured him with a sly smile. "It is all in the tone of voice and manner of suggestion. It is one of the first things we are taught and made to promise we will never divulge. It would be so crass for gentlemen to know we are really asking them. Excuse me."

And with that, she swept away, head held high, moving directly towards Mr. Foyle. Mere moments after that, the gentleman was escorting her to the floor for the next dance.

"Clever girl," Webb murmured with a smile, continuing about the room and wondering if he should also find a partner for the dance. Just for fun.

CHAPTER 11

Dancing was one of the rare forms of entertainment that was almost always acceptable to ladies of station, whether they truly enjoyed it or not.

Rose hated idle chitchat, so she usually unnerved her dance partners with more pressing questions and conversation, and the response from them usually determined if they were worthy of her attention. Years and years of this practice had perfected her way of things, and it was proving rather efficient in her dancing activities this evening.

Everyone was agreeable, she could say that much. But agreeableness was not her primary concern. She had anticipated agreeable guests from the first moment she had met Lady Standhope, and she had yet to be disappointed. Agreeable people, however, were not always intelligent or witty people, let alone ones to whom a marriage might be desirable.

After yet another mediocre dance with a candidate she'd had mild hopes for, Rose made her way to Webb, chatting with Emily and Bertram against one side of the room. They all watched her approach, each expression slightly different from the others.

"No?" Webb asked when she was close enough.

Rose shook her head very firmly. "Mr. Campion seemed to believe that any woman who speaks Latin has extended her brain too far and will likely succumb to insanity before she reaches the age of thirty."

"Not much time for you," Emily replied with a wrinkle of her nose. "What did you tell him?"

Rose smiled very slightly. "*Et ego insaniam,* of course. He was not entirely certain what I meant by it, so perhaps I should offer to tutor him."

They laughed and Webb shook his head, scanning the room further. "Well, he was one of the favorites on our list. How disappointing. How many dances was that, Rose? Six? Seven?"

"Six," she said on a sigh. "I am feeling less and less festive by the moment."

"Take a dance with Bash, then," Emily suggested with a flick of her fingers towards their youngest brother. "He's always worth a laugh or two."

"I'll dance with you, unless you wish for a reprieve," Webb offered with a light shrug before Rose could even look towards Bash. "I'm a better conversationalist, and I actually know about your scheme, so…"

Rose laughed once. "Did this just become a competition?"

"It is *always* a competition with the Rixton brothers," Emily assured her, rolling her eyes. "Webb is probably a better dancer. But don't feel like you have to. Like he said, if you want a reprieve…"

She didn't actually want a reprieve. If she only had to dance with tiresome men, perhaps she might. But her energy was up and the night was young. Webb looked remarkably handsome in his festive ensemble and she had yet to see anyone more pleasing to the eye. Sometimes, it simply suited to dance with a handsome man for no other reason than because he was handsome.

Was that so dreadful a motivation? Besides, he was her

friend. And a handsome friend must be useful for something, mustn't he?

Appreciated for it, at least.

"A dance with you would be most welcome, Webb," Rose told him on an exhale, hoping she looked relieved and not necessarily delighted.

Of course she was delighted, but she did not want him to think more of the delight than he ought. She did not want herself to think more of the delight than there was. It was just a dance with a handsome friend, and someone she could truly converse with. No pretense, no testing questions and interrogations for her ends.

Just her and just him, and that was going to be a relief in and of itself.

Webb was holding his hand out, and Rose belatedly wondered how long he had been doing so, and if her sudden rambling in the mind had distracted her from seeing it. But she took his hand with a warm smile and allowed him to lead her to the floor.

It was another country dance, as seemed to be the theme of the evening, and it was something she was usually grateful for. Plenty of motion and energy, and not an excessive amount of time with only one person's undivided attention.

But she found herself wishing it were something a little slower and more sedate, something that would allow her to talk to him without anyone else listening.

"You're not enjoying yourself," Webb said when they first joined in the dance, taking hands and turning about.

"False," Rose countered, though her tone held a hesitation she knew he would pick up on.

He gave her a hard look, and she only shrugged. "You are not enjoying yourself as much as you would like, then."

She nodded at that as she backed up with the ladies. "True

enough. But constant dancing for a singular purpose isn't something I enjoy."

They stood waiting for the couples on either side of them to move through the motions of the dance.

"Are you constantly thinking about the M word as you are dancing?" Webb inquired.

She found herself nodding again, stepping to her left while he stepped to his right, allowing the couples to take their new places. "How can I not? That is the end goal, is it not?"

Webb heaved an audible sigh and came to her in line with the other gentlemen, taking her hands and slowly turning about again. "That is too much pressure for any one dance. You've got to ask yourself if this is someone you wish to know better, not if this is someone you wish to bind yourself to for the rest of your life. We have several days, Rose. You don't have to get a proposal tonight."

"I know that," she snapped as they returned to their positions. "I cannot help it if I am thinking about the long term as well as the short term. I have specific aims, and not much time to accomplish them."

He raised a brow at her and looped about the man beside him, proceeding down to the third position while she mirrored the action with the ladies alongside her. Then they met in the center and joined hands to progress with a few other couples down the lines.

"Sorry," Rose murmured, gripping his hands hard. "I shouldn't take that tone with you, of all people. I simply don't like this. Any of this. It is not in my nature, and I feel as though I have somehow returned to the awkward, frightened, hopeful girl of my first Season as well as my eager, determined, scheming mama at the same time. And neither of those creatures suit who I truly am now."

"Forcing anything involving the heart is not natural," Webb

assured her, his hold on her hands tightening as well. "Which is why I'm trying to remind you that you don't want that love match everyone else talks about. You only need someone companionable who will leave you alone, yes? I agree, we don't want Mr. Campion and his views of you, but Mr. Prewitt could still be possible, in that sense."

There was something a little distasteful about hearing Webb discuss the men she was considering and analyzing their suitability, but that might have just been the nature of the task to her own ears. Perhaps she hadn't quite accepted what she truly needed to do in order to get what she wanted from her aunt. Marriage had never been Rose's solution to any of her problems, but now it had to be.

"What if he wants children?" she whispered.

Webb jerked a little and they were forced to part in the dance, walking gracefully along the line of others until they were back into their places, then waiting for the other dancers to finish the lines. She could see Webb's face as he stared at her, a mixture of confusion, curiosity, and concern wreathed in his features. She hadn't meant to express that worry of hers at such an inopportune and relatively public moment, but it had just escaped, and now she could not take it back.

How was she going to answer his queries? She barely knew her own mind on the subject. But the door had been opened and she had to walk through it.

She met Webb in the center of the lines, taking his hands and turning yet again. "Do you want children, Rose?" he asked her urgently, his hold on her gentle now.

"I don't know," she admitted. "I used to, but as I have gotten older, I just don't know anymore. I'd thought it lost to me, and if I want that quiet life alone..."

"Your aunt is cruel to make you consider these things in such contrast to her offer," Webb ground out just before they

101

parted and he had to move back to his line. He shook his head while they moved in their lines as part of the dance.

Was Aunt Edith to blame for all of this? Certainly, Rose wouldn't have considered parenthood again without the prospect of marriage, and she hadn't thought about marriage for several years now. She had been more than content with her father's plan of a dowry at five and thirty that would allow her to live as she wished on her own. That had been the future she foresaw for herself, and one she was comfortable with.

The future she had once wanted was now the uncomfortable one, but only because it seemed foreign by comparison. In the most secret heart of her heart, she doubted anyone would *want* her to mother their children. To engage in the behavior that brought about children, about which she knew far more than other unmarried women in England, thanks to the lack of restricted speech among women of her age. She had never been considered a beauty, and perfectly presentable wasn't exactly what a husband looked for in a bedfellow.

But children had been created without any such feelings time and time again, so it did not even warrant consideration on that score.

So why did she consider it? Why did she believe that it mattered? Why did she want to be seen that way if one did not preclude the other?

There were so many aspects to her doubts, and she had not been forced to face any of them in so many years, she had forgotten they existed.

Why were they making themselves known tonight? This ought to have been a delightful night of frivolity, and yet she was contemplating marriage and motherhood and if she wanted to go through with any of this anymore.

"Come here." Webb took her hand and pulled her from the dance, away from all of the lines, movements, and music, away from the onlookers and potential suitors, and over to an unobtrusive corner that was fairly vacant of decorations and guests.

"And now we've made a scene," Rose muttered, widening her eyes as she looked down at her fingertips, shaking her head. Webb scoffed and leaned against the wall. "We have not. No one is looking over here. I am looking right now, and nobody cares that we have left. In fact, someone else just left the dance because he is weaving too much from drink to continue."

That was hardly comforting, in Rose's mind. To leave a dance for emotional reasons was not as understandable as inebriation reasons, but at least there were so many dancers in the assembly rooms that it would be difficult to miss many of them.

"Talk to me," Webb urged in a low voice. "Is all of this too much for you? Are you regretting the scheme, or the party? What?"

"I just…" She exhaled heavily, losing her sight on surprise tears and turning her head away, fighting for control. She felt Webb's hand take hers, but he said nothing, which showed a level of understanding that she was humbled by.

He only waited while she fought for the words.

Swallowing hard, Rose allowed herself to take another breath. "This has all brought back memories and ideas that I had thought long buried. Things I don't even know if I want anymore, but I cannot remember making that decision. It all faded from my mind with every year that passed with no hint of accomplishing them. I became so comfortable with being alone that it became what I wanted. Now that my aunt has forced me to consider matrimony to get what I want, I no longer understand if what I thought I wanted is still what I want, or if what I once wanted is something I still want, and I don't know who I am anymore if I don't want what I want."

She was beginning to panic, her breath coming in deeper

and more rapidly, the crisis of her thoughts and feelings roaring to life even as her words began to make less and less sense as they tumbled out of her mouth. Her mind spun faster than her words, and her heart could not contain all of them. Her tears felt hot against her suddenly frozen cheeks, while her ribs felt too small for her lungs, her body too confining for her sensations.

Webb turned to her fully, taking the hand he held and pressing it against his heart. "Rose... Rose, listen to me. Feel my heart and let it steady you."

She tried, pressing her palm harder against him, willing her skin to absorb each pulse and ground herself in it.

"Breathe with my breath."

She obediently inhaled with him and attempted to keep pace, finding the edge of this terrifying chasm growing less and less defined and the ground beneath her feet more and more stable. Her fingertips almost gripped the skin beneath the layers of Webb's clothing, willing his strength to pass into her in this confounding whirlpool of madness she was currently encased in.

"That's it, Rose. There you are. It's all right." His warm fingers brushed at her cheeks quickly, then smoothed over them with a tenderness that grounded her as much as his steadying heart and calming breath.

Her vision came into better view, though she wasn't certain when she had lost focus, and she locked her eyes on Webb.

His smile was impossibly gentle, bordering on tender, and his free hand cupped her cheek, his thumb still stroking against it. "There you are," he said again, his voice barely a whisper.

Rose inhaled silently, then exhaled and swallowed. "I'm sorry."

"What in the world are you sorry for?" he asked, his palm pressing against her cheek. "I'm grateful you admitted your feelings to me, even if it made you panic. Your torment over all of this is not unfounded, and I have no intention of telling anyone about it, if that was your fear."

"I know you won't," Rose assured him as she shook her head. "I didn't know... Didn't realize that I still cared so much. That any of this mattered. I still don't know how much, but..."

Webb covered her hand, still on his chest, with his own, which effectively silenced her. "You don't have to know," he murmured, his dark eyes suddenly captivating her. "Not until you find yourself wanting to make a decision on a person. You may not even know your mind until that happens, and you have to allow yourself that freedom and opportunity." He curled his fingers around her hand, almost cradling it against him. "Give yourself that grace, Rose."

She found her throat clenching and tried to swallow and smile at the same time. "Perhaps you should be preaching from the pulpit instead of Mr. Alchurch."

Soft laughter wafted over her. "I am all for giving the Almighty credit when it is due, but I am talking about you, Rose Portman, giving Rose Portman the grace to be uncertain and to change her mind about what matters to her. To find happiness wherever it lies for her, even if it is not comfortable."

Rose could barely catch her breath with the passion in his voice, the meaning behind his words, the revelation they were to her ears, and how badly she wanted to do exactly as he said. And then there was the sudden sense that a fire was starting in the hand he held, and she wasn't entirely certain what to do about it. If there was to be anything done about it.

Or if fire was exactly what she needed.

"I will try," Rose whispered with a nod. "I am not sure I can promise more than that."

Webb grinned, her stomach flipping quite dramatically as he did so. "Trying is perfect." He brought her hand to his lips and kissed it rather gently, surprising her.

His eyes flicked upwards. "Mistletoe. Seemed suitable

under the circumstances."

She'd never hated a single word more than mistletoe in that moment.

And hating mistletoe, or any word, had never happened in her entire life.

Curious...

Webb lowered her hand, still holding it. "Still wish to dance?"

With him? Of course. But that would not suit for the moment, given her breathlessness and the dance they had just snuck away from.

"A reprieve from the current one," Rose said in a stronger voice. "And then Bash. Then back to the hunt, but as you said, with less pressure on the thing, and some grace for myself."

Webb nodded in approval, his smile going back to that small one that seemed to heat her from the inside out. "That's my girl. Let's go to it."

His girl? It was on the tip of her tongue to spear him with some sharp words for that, but she hadn't the heart for it.

She actually liked the way it sounded, which was even more curious.

CHAPTER 12

Christmas Eve dawned bright and merry, even for those who had been awake into the early hours of the morning at the assembly rooms.

Webb had never been able to sleep late even when he had been up excessively late, and he simply had to cope with the differences the amount of sleep provided him. This morning's headache was really rather mild, as he hadn't imbibed much the night before, and it made exploring the house much more pleasant.

As did the decorations already being put in place by the staff. He supposed the idea was for the family and guests to awake with the greenery and such already in place, much like a magical change of their scenery while they slept.

He did love watching it all take shape in the corridors and rooms, filling the house with so much beauty and festivity, lifting the spirits as much as the greenery itself was being lifted... Was there this much effort going on at Downing House with what his children, siblings, mother, and staff had put together?

Laughing, Webb shook his head at his own thoughts. It was far too early in the morning for any one of his family members to be involved in anything like decorating. The staff might have begun doing so, but no one else would have.

He entered the painted drawing room, which, as he understood it, was only called such because there were images and designs painted on the walls instead of using wallpaper or a single color. It was part of a collection of other drawing rooms in this portion of the house, and it seemed that all of them had already been furnished with appropriate decoration. And this one, as it happened, also boasted the lovely addition of Rose Portman, for the present.

"What in the world, may I ask, does any house, even one of unconscionable size, need so many drawing rooms for?" he asked with a smile as he moved farther into the room.

Rose turned from the window, looking tired but smiling easily. "I was just wondering the same thing."

Webb found his eyes darting over every aspect of her, looking for any sign of the panicked version he'd encountered at the ball. She hadn't made a reoccurrence last evening, her dancing even taking on a more jovial edge and her face bathed in smiles every time he saw her. They hadn't spoken of her partners much, more for his deciding to avoid the topic in hopes of limiting her stress, but he had wondered...

Well, other than appearing tired, she looked well. Her dark hair was simply pulled up in the sort of chignon his sister liked to wear, and her gown was a fairly simple white muslin, and rather than a shawl, she had a green woolen mantle about her shoulders and arms, which seemed appropriate for the chill he had felt that morning. She was lovely, even like this, and the shade of green enhanced her eyes. They were a pale blue this morning, and he was not sure if that was due to the lack of sleep or the emotions of the night before.

Her lips were pressed in a thin line of a smile, and that, he was sure, was some form of awkwardness she was trying to work through.

He'd make short work of that.

"How did you sleep?" he asked in a softer voice, coming to her.

Rose shrugged. "Fine, considering the amount of time it was. Sleeping late has never been my way, and I have never enjoyed taking a tray in bed, so I thought I would wander the house before I am expected to entertain myself."

"And see the decorations going up?" Webb hinted, indicating the beauty that had been added to the room they were in.

"Yes." Rose looked up, smiling at the greenery. "It is all very elegant. I do find myself wondering how the trimmings at Downing House will compare…"

Webb chuckled, clasping his hands behind his back. "They will compare in enthusiasm, but I fear in little else. I have no doubt they will be constantly readjusted as various aspects fall and sag from their fixed positions."

"But more personal," Rose pointed out. "The children will be so pleased to see their creations up in the house, will they not?"

"I hope so." Webb sighed as he stared out the window, looking in the direction of his home, but unable to see it from this distance. "They'll be finalizing their presents today, and Emily has not indicated the slightest hint to me as to what to expect."

Rose laughed softly. "That makes her an excellent aunt, if a frustrating sister. What surprises truly exist in our adult lives? Let your children surprise you, Webb. For your own sake as well as theirs."

Webb looked at her again, wondering at the almost sentimental tone she was taking on, and given what she had said last evening, he was viewing a much softer version of Rose than he had ever expected. He did not mind this one; in fact, he liked it a great deal and found great comfort in her. But he wanted to know why the change had happened, and if she was also comfortable with it. If she was not, there was no purpose in enjoying the appearance.

"Rose," Webb ventured, turning to lean against the window and stare at her more fully, "are you all right?"

She folded her arms, tucking her mantle more closely to her. "I think so. Thank you for inquiring. I feel a little vulnerable this morning. Not because of you," she added hastily, putting a hand on his arm. "You were wonderful last evening, and so very helpful."

He nodded his thanks but said nothing about it. He did not want to discuss his actions when her emotions were of far more concern.

"Just because of where my mind went," Rose went on. "I didn't realize I cared so much anymore. I have spent so long *not* caring that it became a large part of me. Now that part is less certain, and I feel scrubbed raw. It is most uncomfortable."

"How can I help?" Webb asked, wishing he could hug her in this moment. She deserved a warm embrace, and he would have felt better holding her secure in his arms.

He wouldn't think too closely on that impulse.

Rose patted his arm again, squeezing gently for a moment. "You already are. By being my friend and allowing me to be whoever I am at any moment, I feel some semblance of control and freedom, which helps a great deal. And I would very much like to enjoy Christmas while trying to accomplish my aunt's requirements."

Webb did his best not to rear back in surprise. "You still want to do as she requires?"

He heard a small, almost disbelieving laugh. "I can hardly believe it myself, but yes, I do. I don't know what I am looking for anymore, aside from some intelligence, manners, and respect."

"All fair things," Webb concurred with an approving nod.

"But I do still love the idea of the quiet cottage in the Cotswolds," Rose admitted with a small smile. "Even if I only visit some of the time. It would be just a lovely place for respite."

"Can't argue with that," he quipped. "If it is what you really want."

Rose was already nodding, her smile spreading. "It is. And if my aunt wants me to marry to get it, then I will try to make the best marriage I can, under these circumstances, to get it."

"Right, then," Webb replied, doing his best not to show his surprise at her particularly calm demeanor on the subject. Her acceptance of the task before her, after struggling so much to find and consider her own feelings. He would not pretend that he understood the complicated nature of a woman's feelings, nor of the way in which they were so encouraged to tamp them down by Society. Tamp them down, ignore them, and yet still be considered delicate, fragile, and emotional.

He had heard plenty of the commentary from gentlemen, so called, young and old, who viewed women in such a way. Even their own sisters, which he certainly did not think was fair. Siblings ought to be able to express themselves more freely with each other than with members of Society, and without judgment.

Would it help Webb to look at Rose as he might Emily, then? To tease her as such, let her express herself as such, keep her confidence as such, protect her as such, and help her as such? Would all of this work itself out more neatly if he adopted Rose in such a way?

He watched her as surreptitiously as possible as they both stared out the window, trying not to frown as he did so. Not because looking at her made him frown, but because now he was the one conflicted with what he wanted and what he thought. Now he couldn't see the clearer way forward. Now he needed to examine his ideas for the scheme and try to determine how he would act.

Because Rose was not his sister. He didn't want to see her as his sister. He didn't think he could *ever* treat her like his sister.

She was too intriguing, too lovely, too entertaining, and taking up far too much space in his thoughts to ever be viewed in such a platonic fashion.

And it was the complete lack of platonic feelings at the moment that was giving him quite the fog over concise thought.

She had the faintest impression of freckles in her complexion, and he was fascinated by them. As though she hadn't been bothered to wear bonnets out of doors for the entirety of her adolescence and her complexion had never fully recovered, even if she wore them now. Then there was the very particular shade of blue in her eyes, which he was fairly certain matched the sky in the springtime. Now all he wanted to do was see her eyes in the springtime so he could be sure of their shade.

He wanted to make her laugh. He wanted to laugh with her—laugh until they both shook silently and had tears of mirth leaking from their eyes. He wanted to see the wry curving of her mouth when she was feeling amused in a cynical way, especially if he was having a similar thought. He wanted to be the one she turned to when she cried. Hell, he wanted to hold her when she cried and wipe the tears from her eyes, or let them dry upon his shoulder. Perhaps even kiss them away.

Webb's eyes widened as he focused on some point on the horizon, his throat clenching as though some force were gripping it in hand.

Kiss? Hold?

Aside from being the very opposite of platonic, he had also never had the thought of doing such a thing with anyone except Mary in his entire life. The fact that he was having it now with Rose was both shocking and uncomfortable, aside from the fact that he was actually excited about the idea and felt no shame about it.

None.

No guilt, no shame, no twinge of impulse to run to the cemetery to confess to Mary where his mind was going or feeling like he was forgetting her...

On the contrary, he felt as though Mary was laughing at him.

With him.

Well, if he had been laughing, anyway.

Part of him wanted to, but he was still too traumatized by the suddenness of the thought to even smile.

So instead, Webb swallowed, acknowledging that he could not see Rose in a platonic fashion, let alone as a sister, and tried to focus on the scheme itself. "So did your dancing last night lead to any insights on particular gentlemen? For good or ill—I've no preference so long as the information is detailed."

Rose chuckled in a low, almost throaty manner that did something to the arch of his left foot. Almost as though it wanted to curl inside his boot and his ankle roll until the bone touched the floor.

Bizarre sensation.

"Seeing as I was not judging a man's candidacy based on dancing abilities," Rose began, shifting her weight—Webb flattered himself—to lean a little closer to him, "my thoughts are purely based upon conversation and the manner of the man in question."

"Understood," he confirmed with a nod, willing the tension in his chest to find some other soul to plague until he could get his senses to return. "And very wise. I am a dreadful dancer most of the time."

Rose sputtered and glanced up at him. "You danced well enough with me."

Blast. He'd forgotten that he'd danced with her the night

before. Twice, as it happened, and he had been so focused on her emotional outburst that he recollected absolutely none of it.

Did that make his words a lie?

Thinking quickly, he gave her a wry look, finding bantering with her to be practically habitual and thus not requiring much of his sense. "Perhaps you are not as capable a dancer as you think, and I was passable because of some fault of yours."

She looked almost impressed with his barb, her smile turning coy. "His lordship has some bite with his bark this morning. Not very festive on Christmas Eve."

"Holly has sharp edges to its leaf, does it not?" he replied, hoping he did not need to apologize. "I argue that I am simply a different version of festive."

"Now you're beginning to sound like me," she countered.

Webb shrugged. "There are worse things."

They shared a smile, and again, Webb's left foot tingled. He forced his toes to curl hard, hoping it would drive the sensation away.

"As to the question of gentlemen," Rose said with a soft clearing of her throat, making Webb wonder if she knew how his foot was tingling and that he would need a distraction, "there are a few who have not rendered themselves out of contention due to some poor opinions, ill-judged comments, or sheer stupidity."

Webb snorted a laugh, covering his mouth just for a moment, loving the spice without spite in her voice. It was her manner to be so direct and frank, and to go without softening the hard edges of her own thoughts. He loved the difference between her manner and that of the traditional ladies of Society and loved that there would never be any mistaking the opinions of Rose Portman.

"Mr. Foyle, for example, carries himself well," she went on. "He knows his mind on several topics and does not waste time on idle flattery. What is his situation?"

"Not bad, as it happens." Webb twisted his mouth in thought. "He has a pretty property to the east that has been in his family for generations and brings in perhaps ten thousand a year. As far as I know, he is even-tempered and companionable. He'd certainly make a comfortable match without much fuss."

Rose nodded in approval. "Mr. Greene talks a great deal, but the content is decent. Very polite, but almost too polite. It may not matter, if the marriage is the distant-but-comfortable one I originally envisioned, but I do wonder about the idea of raising children with him, should he wish it."

"Bottom of the list, then." Webb tried not to smile, feeling as though they were analyzing horses in this rather straightforward, factual, practically emotionless conversation. "His father travels extensively, but leaves his mother behind, so you would also have Mrs. Greene to contend with. I know little of her, but nevertheless..."

"Mothers do not like me," Rose told him with a curt shake of her head.

"Mine does." Webb winced very slightly, wishing he hadn't said that. It wasn't about his family, his mother, his likes, wants, or needs...

Not that liking, wanting, or needing was involved here, on his part or otherwise.

But if Rose continued to grin the way she was at this moment, that involvement might just shift.

"Does she?" Rose asked through her wide smile. "I liked her very much, too. But she's used to the four of you and all that you say and do together. I must appear to blend right in with the mix."

She *did* blend in with the rest of them. She fit perfectly, even with Bertram's dry humor tossed in. She was as perfect a fit with them as Mary had been, but his wife had known them all for several years before marrying in. Her style of humor had been

115

mostly deflecting the madness of the Rixton siblings and sighing in amusement at their antics. She had been the peacemaker, the one every person tried to get on their side for victory and sense, the gentling influence on all of them.

Rose could not be more different, and yet not incompatible or wrong in any way. She was an active participant in the banter and antics, challenging where she wanted and ignoring where she did not. If she were to be a regular fixture in such sibling settings, she would be the one they wanted on their side as a weapon, not a shield. Victory might be assured with her because of her very specific arsenal, and the perfect nettles she was capable of.

But Rose also had a large heart—tucked among the brambles she had planted over the years, it was true, but he had seen it there. He had seen it with the children, and he had seen it in her conversation with his mother. Rose couldn't have known that his mother would have such a commentary on her children, and it had been some time since she had said anything of the sort in the company of others. That she had done so was a sign of her trust in and comfort with Rose, and to accomplish that in so short a time...

Webb couldn't tell Rose any of this though. He could barely think it without a sense of panic coming over him. It was far too soon for any of this to be occurring to him. Not in regards to Mary's death—he felt he was comfortably removed enough there to consider feelings for someone else—but with barely knowing Rose a few days and already thinking...

It was much too soon. It was only the close proximity and compressed amount of time in that proximity. Some time at home away from her would certainly help him to regain some sanity and sense, as well as reality.

She was a friend and ally, and his noticing additional things about her and feeling certain ways was surely just an indication that he truly was ready to consider taking a wife in the future. It couldn't be Rose, specifically, this quickly.

It just couldn't be.

"Who else?" Webb asked through a slightly tightened throat, willing his panic to fade. "Who else is on the list, I mean. Or off it."

"Alchurch, bless him, is off," Rose admitted with a heavy sigh. "I like him immensely, but he deserves a wife who matches his goodness and doesn't contemplate running away to a cottage in the Cotswolds. Someone content to remain with him at all times, if he wishes it. I just do not see myself filling that role. While we're at this house party, I may dance with him more than once purely as a respite, but he cannot be my husband."

Why was that such a relief for Webb to hear? Alchurch wasn't his competition for Rose's affections, and he wasn't even pursuing Rose's affections.

Was he?

Rose wasn't sure she wanted her affections involved in any of this, she had said so herself. If Webb did have affections involved, would there be anything worse than knowing hers were not? He would need to watch himself, or he would be setting himself up for a lifetime of heartache and longing for more.

If that was what he was feeling, of course. Once he knew, then he could adjust his plans accordingly.

"Mr. Harris would be a candidate," Rose went on, oblivious to Webb's thoughts, "but Mrs. Richards is fixed on pairing him with Miss Proffitt, and I am not about to get in the way of her plans. She might then get ideas for me, and I cannot bear that thought."

Neither could Webb. Making a match for Rose was something he had committed to do, and suddenly he couldn't bear the thought of that either. But if he stuck to their plan, Rose could have the comfortable, distant marriage she had originally wanted, and he would know that no one held her heart.

There was something bittersweet about that, but it was all Webb could do for the moment.

It would have to be enough.

CHAPTER 13

Christmas Eve had always been a time of decoration and games for Rose in the past, and the occasional ball, but as they had all attended the ball at the assembly rooms the night before, Lady Standhope seemed content with letting the day be one of feasting and entertainment. There had been a brief trip for some to the church to set up decorations, but Rose had not gone along with them. Considerate as Mr. Alchurch was, she did not wish to pretend she cared how the place of worship was adorned for services in the morning.

It was a poor clergyman indeed who could make his parishioners more focused on the manner of decoration within the church than the sermon being given from its pulpit on Christmas Day.

While the church decorating had been going on, Rose had enjoyed some quiet reading in the expansive library at Fairview. It had been the most leisurely thing she had managed for the entire house party, and she loved the lack of outside participation required. She could ignore her own thoughts and lose herself in the world of her novel, and with every turned page, she felt her mind and body relax further and further still.

Perhaps if she spent the remainder of the house party reading, she would enjoy the entire thing more.

Truth be told, not all of it was dreadful. Webb had been a saving grace in so many respects, and she already owed him an immense debt for his actions the night before. He had calmed her so sweetly, so effectively, that it was as if he had known exactly what she needed, as if he had calmed her before. But she had never felt panic or overwhelmed like that before, so she couldn't have told anyone how to help her, let alone someone she had only known for a few days. And dancing with him had been her favorite parts of the night, if she were to be perfectly honest. She did not have to watch her words or her steps, did not have to think strategically or be particularly observant.

She could just *be*.

Perhaps that was her favorite part about being with Webb. She felt like herself, and she felt safe enough to be herself. When had she last been able to say that about anyone? She was mostly herself around her siblings and her cousins, but even they did not know the whole of her.

Webb, obviously, did not know the whole of her either, but she wouldn't mind if he did.

Rose shook her head now as her maid set her hair in a pinned coif of curls. She was starting to plan significant portions of her day around Webb, and that was not going to help her find the husband she needed to for Aunt Edith. She needed to set aside her own enjoyment and focus on the task at hand.

Why was that so difficult to remember? She had given up the idea of a real marriage and of love, hadn't she? Years ago, she had given it all up when it was clear that she was simply not the sort of woman who men viewed in such a light. Yet here she was, trying to craft the perfect marriage of convenience and unable to let go of the most girlish idea at the core of any woman in the world.

That had been what had set her off last night with her tears and panic, and tonight it was simply leaving her depressed and discouraged.

What would Webb have to say when he found out?

It would be as though he did not know Rose Portman at all, and he would probably consider her to be an overly emotional shrew who lashed out when provoked in even the slightest way. Even he would want to distance himself after that, and she would be left alone to try and manage this foolishness without help.

"Anything else, Miss Portman?" her maid asked, meeting her eyes in the mirror.

Barely looking at her reflection, Rose shook her head. "No, thank you. I shall go down now."

The maid bobbed and left the room, leaving Rose with her thoughts.

She needed to ask Webb to tell her who wouldn't want children among the group. She liked children immensely, but she did not want to have any of her own if there was no real affection between herself and her husband. It just did not seem fair to raise a family that way, not with how Rose wanted to live. And choosing to live that sort of marriage was well within her rights, as she saw things. Wives were allowed a certain level of independence, and that was all she wanted.

A good man with sensible prospects who wanted nothing of her.

That would save her from the heartache she feared, the rejection she had felt, and the vulnerability she wished to avoid.

With a nod, Rose picked up her gloves and slid the first on her right hand as she made her way out of the room, starting down the corridor.

She heard a faint hissing behind her and turned in surprise.

Webb was walking towards her, grinning and giving her a slight wave.

Why was that the most adorable thing she had ever seen in her entire life? And why was he so bleeding handsome that it actually hurt her chest when he smiled?

Her eyes widened at the realization, and she did her best to force a smile in spite of it.

Webb gave her a cautious look. "What? You look...something."

"That's an astute description," Rose retorted, jamming her left hand into her glove awkwardly. "I look something. Although it probably ought to be 'some way' to be grammatically correct, don't you think?"

"Undoubtedly," Webb concurred. He seemed to relax slightly with her reply and offered his arm to her.

Rose looked at it for a moment, then met his eyes. "Why?"

Webb blinked. "Because...we're walking and going downstairs to the others? Because we're walking side by side and it's a gentlemanly thing to do? Because we're friends and you look lovely and I'd feel like a heel if I didn't? Because...I want to?"

Now it was Rose who just blinked, staring at him and feeling rather like a heel herself. Were her defensive thoughts now going to make their way to defensive actions, even with him?

"Oh," she eventually said, her voice dipping low. "All right, then." She hooked her hand through his arm and started walking beside him.

"Do you always treat gallantry as offensive?" Webb asked her, seeming truly curious.

"I'm not offended," Rose muttered, averting her eyes.

She heard a scoffing sound that made her cheeks burn. "You need to work on your acting skills, Rose. I thought you were going to strike me for offering you my arm. Heaven knows what you would have done if I'd thrown my cloak over a puddle in your path."

As though determined to prove him correct, her stomach dropped and her heart lurched and her jaw tensed, her mind spinning on any number of retorts.

But then she felt the steadiness of his arm beneath her hand, inhaled the faintest scent of sandalwood, pine, and sage from him, and everything within her, from head to toe, was soothed in a gentle wave of warmth.

This was Webb. He was safe, and so was she. There was no need to overreact, and she ought to be working on doing as he suggested the night before and give herself some grace.

And breathing room to simply be, just as he did for her.

"I don't hate gallantry," she told him in a clear voice. "I hate the implication that a woman cannot do something or requires the assistance of a man. That I might need someone to steady me while I walk, for instance."

"There are other reasons to offer a lady my arm," Webb pointed out without any sort of defensiveness or spite.

Rose nodded as they turned the corner, moving towards the stairs. "I know. Sometimes it is simply for the purpose of escorting a body somewhere for politeness."

"And sometimes it's a mark of respect or deference," Webb added, nudging her side with his elbow. "Sometimes it's a symbol of affection. And sometimes..." He paused, looking around, and then leaned close. "Sometimes it's because fashion requires the skirts of ladies to be so bleeding long that even the most graceful can trip on them if not mindful. Believe me, I've had to catch Emily on the stairs more than once because of skirts, and she is nothing if not graceful."

There was something about Webb being closer to her and practically whispering that raised bumps along every inch of exposed skin, and a few inches of unexposed skin, cascading ripples along her entire frame as though she had been licked by a particularly poignant fire. A blissful, light, holly-and-mistletoe-bedecked fire.

And now the fire was racing into her cheeks, and it was difficult to breathe, let alone laugh at the image of Emily nearly tumbling down the stairs.

Still, she managed to choke out something that resembled laughter and fanned herself, not for amusement, but for the desperate need of a cooler breeze.

"Skirts," Webb repeated, mistaking Rose's guttural sounds for actual laughter. "Dangerous creations. So really, this is for your safety more than my own amusement. But for both our sakes, I'll release your arm before we join the others. Neither of us need to have this mistaken for an understanding, do we?"

Rose shook her head, feeling rather stupid and slow, but as his words played over again in her mind, beginning to feel doused in chilled water. She shivered from the effects, a few stubborn embers still alight deep in the pit of her stomach, in spite of the dousing.

"No," she said for emphasis. "Now we know there are two eager and sharp-eyed matchmakers in the house, it would behoove us both to be vigilant. Can you imagine what would happen if word leaked to the village about something between us? Fred and Bash would ride up to the house and demand an explanation of some sort."

Webb chuckled even as his arm stiffened beneath her hand. "They would, but more because they would be finding out by rumor than from either of us. Those two have a more vested interest in gossip than any woman I have ever met."

"I have always found that men are just as interested in gossip as ladies," Rose told him with a sniff, starting down the stairs and gliding one gloved hand along the railing. "It is simply less spread about. I know very well that is what you all discuss in your clubs."

"No!" Webb gasped rather dramatically, making her snort with true laughter. "Who told you? We are sworn to secrecy from the moment we leave school never to reveal what goes on in there! Tell me his name, I'll have his membership and his blade!"

Rose shook her head, retreating into the safety of pointless banter while she adjusted to the varied sensations coursing through her. "No, I am bound by the code of blood, and I shall not divulge the identity of my source."

"Ah-ha! So they're related to you!" He barked a laugh of faux superiority. "That will cut the list down by several counts. You have no brothers, and brothers-in-law are not bound by blood. Now I simply need to know how many uncles and male cousins you have, and I will work the culprit out and have my vengeance."

"Oh, do calm down, it was probably Richard." Rose laughed.

Webb narrowed his eyes. "Richard who? Tell me his surname, or I will be forced to seek out all the Richards in England."

"You would make a terrible villain," she told him, unable to keep the smile from her face.

Webb's laughter was far more natural now. "Terrible as in...?"

Rose rolled her eyes. "As in not a very successful one. You would be incapable of villainy."

"I very much beg your pardon." Webb sniffed dismissively as they reached the bottom of the stairs. "I could be an excellent villain with the right amount of practice and a provoking motivation. I think anyone could be a decent victim with those, actually."

"More than likely. But you're not the villainous type, Webb." Rose shook her head, smiling without feeling the need to look at him while she did so. "You are far too nice a person. Far too affable in genuine ways, and not at all inclined to think evil of anyone. I rather think you'd be the sort to save the world than to wish it ill."

Webb was silent a long moment, and Rose wondered if she might have said too much or simply made him uncomfortable. She hadn't meant to be effusive in praise, simply honest. And she honestly felt that way about Webb and his nature, but it was not the sort of thing that a lady usually said to a gentleman. Or a woman to a man. Even if they were friends, it might have been too much.

Rose might have been too much.

"I genuinely do not know how to respond to that," Webb finally said, all traces of humor and teasing gone. "It may be the kindest thing anyone has ever said, and I would refute every point of it in the interest of self-deprecation, but I know your tendency to be honest rather than flatter, and if that is your perception of me… Rose, I don't know what to say other than to thank you."

He had not lowered his arm, but she had not released it either, and with the way her heart was pounding at the moment, it seemed unwise to try.

"I did not say it for your gratitude," Rose murmured, her eyes flicking to him. "It is simply the truth."

"Your truth," he pointed out, smiling a little. "I cannot refute your perception, but do consider that reality may not match it."

There it was. Webb would find some way to tell her she was wrong without actually saying so, and the neatly placed correction had been inserted with precision.

Rose let herself sigh in exasperation that was only superficial. "I choose to live in my perceptions, Webb. Heaven knows what I appear to be in reality."

"Would you like me to tell you?"

His offer came in a low, rumbling tone that reignited the fire in her, roaring to life across her skin and destined to make itself known on her face.

They were at the Grand Drawing Room now, where everyone was gathered for the beginning of the evening's activities and entertainment, and still they were arm in arm. Rose was suddenly acutely aware of the exact distance between their bodies, and the sheer heat that emanated from him, practically burning the entire length of her.

"Later, perhaps," she whispered, afraid to look him in the eye, unsure of what she would find there and what he might see in her eyes.

She was barely breathing, her pulse thundering in her ears, and the idea of hearing something that would possibly make those things worse...

She'd be torn between fleeing the evening entirely and retiring to her bedchamber and finding a comfortable spot of equal burning inside one of the fires in Fairview. It might be less painful than the vulnerability of moving forward.

"We should go in," she continued quickly, removing her hand from his arm and clearing her throat in what could only be described as an awkward and obvious manner. "Heaven knows what awaits us, and I will need your assistance in narrowing the field. I must concentrate my efforts if I am to succeed."

"Yes, you must," Webb agreed as he reached for the door, his tone returned to his usual one. "Have you spoken with Lady Standhope at all? I'd hate to think what she is telling your aunt of her own volition."

It occurred to Rose that she ought to have shuddered at the thought herself, but all she could feel at this moment was a desperation to not be aware of every fiber of her being and every freckle on her skin with shocking clarity.

"I should speak with her," she murmured absently as they

entered the room, her eyes immediately finding their hostess, who was wearing a sly smile. "Perhaps tomorrow."

"Not right now?" Webb asked, clasping his hands behind his back.

Rose shook her head slowly, heart sinking. "I have a feeling she would be more inclined to mischief tonight, and mischief is the very last thing I need."

CHAPTER 14

Well, this was certainly the most unusual Christmas Eve that Webb had ever experienced.

First, there had been the long sword dancers and their exceptional performance, which had garnered rather appropriately impressive reactions from the guests. Webb had seen them before, of course, as it was a bit of a local tradition, but it had been some years since he'd had the pleasure of their performance. It was always worth watching the expressions of those who were not local for such a thing. The awe mingled with terror was particularly amusing, and it had been no exception tonight.

Then there had been an arranged timing of a group of local wassailers, which had been a pleasant enough diversion. Their music had been particularly stirring, and they had ended their performance with some of the more jaunty local tunes, which had brought on some improvised dancing from a few of the guests.

Not Rose, he'd noted with a hint of satisfaction. He wouldn't have objected to her dancing, as he was not in a position to do so and it might actually have given him pleasure, but it would be her choice of partner and the unplanned nature of it all that might have irked him. It was hard to say, really. Rose's list was whittling down, and there was some good and bad associated with that.

After the wassailers had departed, they'd had a relatively reserved supper, which Webb suspected was due to the great feast that their hostess had planned for Christmas Day. Rose had been unusually quiet during the meal, and Webb hadn't pressed her to keep up a conversation. Something was changing between them, and until either of them acknowledged that, whatever it was would hang between them like a low and heavy cloud.

Now they were back in the Grand Drawing Room, and Lady Standhope had announced that there would be ghost stories told.

It was an old tradition in York, stories of a haunted nature during the Christmas season, but Webb had never participated in it. Mostly because his mother despised anything of a supernatural nature and did not enjoy being scared on purpose, but that was neither here nor there. He doubted Lady Standhope would have selected ghost stories that would be truly terrifying, given the delicate nature of a few of the ladies she had invited.

Or perhaps she was the sort who would enjoy having her guests intentionally afraid and jumping at the slightest sounds and desperate for additional candles to be lit.

He'd heard of stranger behaviors in ladies of her age and station.

"Can we not perform a theatrical instead?" one of the young ladies asked in a very small voice as a few candles were doused.

Lady Standhope gave her a sympathetic look. "We will, dear child, in a few days. This is merely a tradition, and my late husband always told the best ones. Do not fear, none of these stories are true." But there was an almost sinister smile on her lips that would reassure no one of that.

Webb shook his head, fighting a smile of his own. The woman was vicious, and now the young lady would wonder about the veracity of these stories all night long.

Rose sat quietly in the middle of a sofa, the seat to her left available, while the one on her right was occupied by Lady Clarke, who was saying something to her with great earnestness. That made Webb blanch slightly. Did he really want to tempt the matchmaker by sitting beside Rose in a darkened room? On the other hand, did he really want anyone else to sit beside her? He looked around the room for Mrs. Richards, who was in eager conversation with Mr. Alchurch.

Now Webb felt his pulse skip a beat or two. Were the women plotting to put the two together? He already knew how Rose felt about Alchurch, but if she were convinced that he would make a good match, and she only wanted something convenient... Would she be so easily persuaded? He did not know these ladies well, nor was he aware of how Alchurch felt about Rose, or marriage in general.

What if Alchurch could convince Rose that her preferred arrangement suited him?

Webb's feet were moving before he knew what he was about, and he cleared his throat very softly when he reached Rose. "Is this seat taken, Miss Portman?"

Rose glanced up at him, her lips quirking to one side, the darkening light in the room making her eyes an almost hypnotic shade of purple. "No, my lord. Please, take it."

Webb swallowed and did so, then looked around her and nodded at Lady Clarke. "My lady, it is very fine to see you this evening."

Lady Clarke smiled at him, propping her walking stick in front of her and resting her hands upon its top. "And you, my lord. Are you prepared for ghost stories?"

Shrugging, Webb put his hands on his knees. "I hope so, though I trust I may count on you to revive me should it all become too much and I swoon."

Lady Clarke chortled, tapping her stick against the floor a little. "What makes you think I have smelling salts upon my person, young man? Am I really so delicate in appearance?"

"Not at all, my lady," Webb countered easily. "I simply believe you to be prepared for all emergencies. You might also have a flask of brandy in that reticule of yours, as well as a dagger concealed in a very sensible boot. One can never be too careful these days."

Rose covered her mouth to stifle giggles while Lady Clarke only shook her head, smiling at him. "Cheeky devil. Do let me know when you are ready for a wife. I shall take great pleasure in finding you one."

"Thank you, my lady. I shall." Webb nodded his thanks and sat back, exhaling slowly.

"Nicely done," Rose whispered, pretending to adjust her gloves. "That is one way to throw them off the scent."

Webb nearly asked how she had known, but the question became caught in his throat. "And you?" he managed.

Rose's smile spread very slightly. "Apparently, I am not even a thought. There are no elderly widowers who wouldn't mind a wife who isn't barely out of leading strings, so I am merely a source of support and confidence for them."

Relief had never tasted so sweet, though there was a distinct hint of Madeira to it, if his mouth were any indication.

Certain Rose would hear the pounding of his heart in his throat, Webb folded his arms and tried to lean away without looking as though he was leaning away. "Why is Mrs. Richards talking to Alchurch so intently?" he asked, not feeling the need to keep his voice as lowered now.

"Lady Clarke was just explaining that to me," Rose informed him, her tone resuming its usual timbre. "May I tell him, my lady?"

"Yes, yes, of course," Lady Clarke said with a flick of her

fingers. "His thoughts would be most welcome."

"For whatever they might be worth," Webb muttered for Rose alone.

She ignored that and turned to him slightly, her eyes a trifle scolding. "The ladies believe that Miss King would make a good match for Mr. Alchurch."

The burst of delight in the pit of Webb's stomach was a sensation he was entirely unprepared for, and he dealt with it by crossing one leg over the other and exhaling slowly. "Really?" he replied, as though it were a deeply interesting thought.

He could feel Rose's eyes on him, but he did not dare meet her gaze.

"You don't have the faintest idea who she is, do you?" There was no question in her voice, but there was a derisive hint of humor that he found frightfully encouraging, all things considered.

"Not a jot," he said at once. "But I support the idea in full."

Rose made a strange humming sound that could have been a new version of her laughter, and he wanted so badly to inquire after it, but now was not the time. Still, it was a delightful shade of sound from her lips and seemed to ring through him like the striking of a gong.

But with far more pleasure.

"She's the quiet beauty in green sitting by Mrs. Dawes," Rose told him, gesturing very faintly in the general direction. "Barely three and twenty, from a good family near Bradford, and a dowry of seven thousand pounds, it is expected. Lovely singing voice and even better at the harp and pianoforte. I suspect we'll hear from her tomorrow during musical performances."

"Is that what is taking place tomorrow? Lovely." Webb nodded in approval, barely sparing a glance for the figure of Miss King. Oh, he recognized her once she had been pointed out, but only as a face of the party and not for any meaningful conversation or context. And if the ladies thought she would make a good wife for Alchurch, who was he to argue the point? He was not interested in making matches, unless they were for Rose, and he trusted that Alchurch, being in possession of a good heart and charitable soul, would make a fine match for himself and for the parish. If that person happened to be Miss King, then good for them all, and especially for the ladies taking pride in the match.

Rose huffed a little beside him. "Honestly, you could pretend to care."

"Why?" he asked in a low voice. "If Alchurch starts pursuing her based on the recommendations of the ladies, then, as the head of a family within the parish, I will care immensely. But I'm not here to marry off my clergyman. I shall watch his actions with interest, but you can hardly expect me to enjoy match speculation."

"You enjoy my speculation," Rose murmured in a voice that Lady Clarke hadn't a hope of hearing.

"No, I don't," he murmured back. "But I've agreed to help you, and so I will."

"What do you—?"

Her question was cut off by Lady Standhope clearing her throat and standing before the fire, a book in her hands. "Our first installment of the night, ladies and gentlemen, is the telling of *Sir Gawain and the Green Knight*. A few of us will read, as it is quite long, and I encourage all who have agreed to read with me to engage in your best theatrics."

"Oh, I am certain that will help it to be less boring," Lady Clarke grumbled, her walking stick making a faint skidding sound against the wooden floor. "This one isn't scary at all, unless you are scared of alliterative verse and a vapid imagination."

Webb choked on laughter and immediately coughed to cover it, gesturing for a footman to bring him a glass of something. Rose was humming again, but this time between shaky breaths, and he could feel the slight trembling of her form as well as see the tension in her lips.

"My lady," she hissed, her words unsteady, "you will make us a spectacle if we laugh during a ghost story."

"Just tell them you laugh when frightened," Lady Clarke retorted without concern. "Might get you out of here faster."

Rose turned towards Webb and hid her face in the shadow his shoulder provided. "I cannot... I am going to..."

He was struggling not to laugh himself and remained as composed as he could, though having Rose so near him was adding to the trouble and making his face warm. "Steady on," he whispered. "Once people start reacting, we should be safe."

"What if they don't? What if everyone is stoic and silent?" She looked up at him, barely a handsbreadth away from his face, and if he turned towards her, he could brush his lips against hers without any effort at all.

Gads, what an impulse to have to fight at this very moment, aflame as he was and already in a darkened space.

"Then," he said through gritted teeth, his hands clenching into fists as they were tucked in his folded arms, "we will literally bite our tongues until they bleed and laugh later."

Rose exhaled slowly, the feeling of it catching at Webb's skin just above his collar.

Hell's teeth...

Then she blessedly straightened and resumed her proper posture, attention forward, entirely composed.

Webb, on the other hand...

Lady Standhope began the reading of *Sir Gawain*, and as she had begged of others, she was very theatrical in doing so. Her cadence was a bit stilted, but one had to give her credit for attempting to alter her voice for each character and changing the volume of it to make things more frightening at times. The trouble

135

with Lady Standhope's rendition was that her voice did not sink particularly low, and so her attempts to sound haunting only served to give her voice a chirping note, which was not at all frightening.

Rose, in particular, seemed to find the voice more amusing than anything else, if the amount of shaking beside Webb was any indication.

"Really, Miss Portman," Lady Clarke whispered for their group only. "If you cannot maintain more decorum, you ought to remove yourself from the space. One cannot tell if you are about to swoon from fright or burst into hysterics."

It was not entirely fair for Lady Clarke to provoke Rose in such a way, as it only served to make the entire situation worse. One slight glance at Rose revealed that her lips were clamped together so hard that they were white, her eyes filled with mirth that threatened to spill over into actual tears.

"I may have need of smelling salts after all," Lady Clarke muttered with a shake of her head, her own lips quirking very slightly.

The woman was utterly devious, and Webb was convinced she actually wished for Rose to burst out laughing just to change the scene before them.

Mr. Garner took over reading after Lady Standhope and, while Webb found the man insufferable in conversation and opinion on a personal level, his skills in the dramatic arts were evident. He was far more able to portray the haunting nature of the tale and to create a variety in voice and characterization of those he read.

The tale of Sir Gawain was one that Webb had heard before, so he paid little attention to it. If Rose had heard it before, he could not tell. She continued to struggle against laughter, though it wasn't as pronounced for Mr. Garner's version. She did not react as shockingly as the rest when Sir Gawain met the Green Knight once more, nor when the axe had to be brought down a second and third time. She did gasp when the identity of the Green Knight was revealed, and she applauded with everyone else when Mr. Garner finished, but without much enthusiasm.

"Is it just me," Rose inquired softly through a false smile, "or did Mr. Garner seem to stay up there for an exceptionally long time for his turn rather than have someone else join in?"

Webb glanced about the room quickly and did see a slightly disgruntled expression on a face or two, including that of Lady Standhope. Stifling laughter, he nodded once. "You would not deny the man his chance to display his great acting and orating skills, would you? He is angling for a leading role in the theatrical, whenever that takes place."

"Remind me to have a headache that evening," Lady Clarke muttered without clapping.

Webb and Rose shared a look, then quickly averted their gaze, laughter threatening to spill over yet again.

Had any evening of ghost stories ever been so entertaining?

"Well," Lady Standhope announced, rising swiftly, "that was quite the rousing rendition, was it not?" Without waiting for additional applause, she went on. "We will now hear the tale of *Beowulf*. Mr. Kent, if you would begin."

Mr. Kent, a rather stout man who was attending the party with his wife and children, stood with a book in hand, clearing his throat excessively.

"Should I anticipate something exceptional based on that?" Rose inquired mildly. "Or simply something of a cold?"

"*Beowulf* always sounds better with congestion," Lady Clarke answered before Webb could do so. "Even better if the reader coughs himself into apoplexy and ends the misery early."

Webb looked around Rose in exasperation at the older woman. "Really, my lady, why did you come down for the reading this evening if you despise these so?"

Lady Clarke returned his look with mild superiority. "How was I to know which stories would have been selected? I love a good haunting. I tend to hope my late sister will appear afterwards. She promised me a set of her jewels that has never materialized, and I am determined to have them."

Rose snorted, covering her mouth and nose quickly, squeezing her eyes shut and breathing very slowly. Webb could only grin and shake his head as he settled in for a mediocre recitation of an epic poem he'd never been particularly fond of.

Mr. Kent was followed by Mr. Greene and Mr. Fellowes, and thankfully that was the end of it. None of the three were particularly dramatic, which seemed to make Lady Standhope quite put out, based on her facial expressions and faint huffing sounds.

"Have you spoken with our hostess this evening?" Webb asked Rose as they applauded for the finishing of Mr. Fellowes's reading.

Rose nodded once. "Before supper. She hopes I am enjoying myself and meeting plenty of her gentlemen guests, and asked if any had met my particular fancy as yet."

Roughly four of Webb's ribs went numb at that. "And?" he pressed as gently as he possibly could under the circumstances. "What did you tell her?"

"I asked her outright if she would tell my aunt what I told her," Rose replied, surprising him with her frankness, but also by how bold it was to ask such a question of their hostess. "She said she would, as it was her sworn duty as her friend."

"Who swears their friends to things like that?" Webb wondered aloud as feeling returned to his chest.

Rose ignored his question. "So I told her that it would not be appropriate to relay information to my aunt that I have yet to decide upon, and if it would not offend her, that I would keep such information to myself until I was more certain."

It was the most perfect response he could have thought of, even if it was a delaying tactic on her part. If such a statement made its way into the content of a letter to Aunt Edith, it would show that Rose was taking the task seriously and also using caution and discretion. Her aunt would be curious, if her taste for gossip was as ravenous as Rose claimed, and would now want to know anything that Rose would share at any time.

"Excellent response," he praised when he was able. "I approve."

"Thank you. You should." Rose tossed her head a little, craning her neck from side to side. "It is the truth, after all. I have decided nothing, and I need to be more certain. She cannot argue with that."

Webb was desperate to ask what specifically she needed to be more certain of, but their hostess was rising again, and he had to bite back a sigh of impatience.

"For our last ghost story of the evening," Lady Standhope announced, her voice now sounding strained, "we will indulge in a bit of local lore. Mr. Ross will favor us with three tales of ghosts from the records of our very own Byland Abbey."

There were sounds of hushed awe from the guests, several of them leaning forward or scooting closer to the front.

"Where is Byland Abbey?" Rose whispered.

Webb scoffed just a little. "To the north, not too far from Thirsk. Having her call it our very own is a stretch, but it is in the county."

"Well, there is that, at least."

"Now these I will attend to," Lady Clarke announced for their little group, seeming to settle in. "I suggest you both do the same, or else Lady Standhope might require something further of us to sate her whims. Heaven knows what that might entail." She shuddered and rested her hands atop her walking stick again, eyes fixed on Mr. Ross.

Rose glanced at Webb with a slight smile, which danced more in her eyes than on her lips, and then also looked forward for the beginning of the tales.

Attend to the story? When a woman with dancing eyes and a beguiling smile sat so close he could inhale the scent of juniper, peppermint, lilies, and honey without any effort whatsoever?

Not bloody likely.

But he would try.

CHAPTER 15

Rose inhaled deeply as she exited the church the next morning, feeling rather satisfied with the length and content of the Christmas Day service. Mr. Alchurch was indeed a capable, charismatic speaker and his reminders about the Christian virtues of charity, faith, hope, and love were timely as well as apt. He did not drone on about any of the aspects, and made practical applications for each, emphasizing the humanitarian generosity that was so welcome to the less fortunate during the present season.

It did not sound like preaching coming from Mr. Alchurch. It sounded like a reasonable discourse with some well-thought-out ideas.

If Rose had anything with her to offer the poor at the moment, she might have wandered the village and done something about it. As she was only visiting, she would hope that Lady Standhope would allow them to help somehow tomorrow on St. Stephen's Day, when gifts and goods were given to tenants and servants.

The day was bright and clear, just as Rose preferred in the winter, and the air was crisp and held notes of the fresh pine from within the church now behind her. It was a delicious feeling, and her heart felt lighter than it had in days. This was the beauty and magic of Christmas, she supposed. She did not wish to be home with her family, but her thoughts did turn to them and to fond memories of Christmases past with her immediate family, extended family, and sweet gifts she had received from her sisters' children not so long ago.

A Christmas walk, Rose decided as she waited in the small line to greet Mr. Alchurch after the service. That was what she wanted to do when they returned to the house and everyone dispersed to their various activities. As she understood matters, nothing would happen of any significance until much later, when the feast would take place and some music and dancing would transpire afterwards.

On such a beautiful day, with such nostalgic feelings, in a lovely setting like this, how could she not embrace the chance to walk about in it?

She smiled at Mr. Alchurch as she reached him. "Lovely service, Mr. Alchurch. One of the best I've heard on Christmas."

He inclined his head, putting a hand to his heart. "Thank you, Miss Portman. Coming from a woman as frank as you, I take that as a deep compliment. May God be with you this Christmas Day."

Rose dipped her chin in a quick nod. "And with you, sir." She moved on, knowing others would wish to give more effusive praise and desperate to get back to spending the day according to her own tastes and dictates.

"Miss Portman."

Webb's voice sent warm ripples down her spine, and she had to crane her neck before turning with a smile, seeing his children on either side of him, their hands in his, and the rest of his family following behind.

She'd forgotten that this was the local church for Downing

House and thus would have all of the Rixtons in attendance this morning.

She did not have to force a smile for any of them.

"Good morning," Rose greeted, returning Kitty's small wave. "Happy Christmas."

"And to you," Lady Downing replied with a warm smile. She was holding little Susan in her arms, and the girl was far more interested in her grandmother's necklace than anything else.

Rose looked at Webb quickly, his smile particularly warm with his children beside him. "I presume you are going home to Downing for the day."

He nodded, his smile spreading. "For most of it, yes. I will return to Fairview for Lady Standhope's feast this evening. We are having an early dinner at Downing so the children can be fully involved."

"That sounds delightful." Rose smiled at each of the children in turn. "You must all be so excited."

"Why don't you join us?" Webb suggested brightly.

Rose looked at him in shock. "On Christmas Day? Webb, this is time for your family."

"And were your family here, I would understand taking the time to be with them instead," he allowed. "But they are not. So why not join us? If you would prefer solitude, then, of course, return to Fairview with our compliments. But if you would like to eat two feasts today..." He trailed off, shrugging but still giving her an almost daring, cheeky smile.

He was inviting her in front of the children, which was entirely unfair. She bit her lip, torn between wanting to smack him for not asking her privately and wanting to hug him for thinking of her when he was going to celebrate with his family.

Webb raised a brow at her, apparently amused by her hesitation. "Come," he murmured encouragingly, seeming to be asking without inflecting his tone in the usual way.

She could almost hear the word "please" following after. It was written in his eyes and held in the curve of his smile.

"Oh, very well," Rose relented, smiling down at the children. "But only because I am very hungry and cannot wait."

Molly and Kitty cheered, making her heart warm so sweetly, she wondered if it were actually stretching within her.

She looked at Lady Downing with a hesitant smile. "Will this dress be suitable enough? I can fetch something nicer from Fairview if you are all changing for dinner."

"Don't you dare," Lady Downing scolded. "You look beautiful, and perfectly appropriate for Christmas dinner with our family." She nodded in the direction of a path. "It is a lovely walk to the house from here. And it will help to tire the children out."

"Shh! Mother!" Bash put a finger to his lips as they started to walk. "You are not supposed to reveal the master plan to those affected by it!"

"I meant you, dear," his mother shot back at once.

Emily and Webb positively howled with laughter, while Fred made a tally mark in the air as though keeping score for his mother. Bertram, carrying his hefty son Dominic, only shook his head with a fond smile.

Rose walked beside Lady Downing, feeling it might be safer than walking with Webb, and wanting to give his children the chance to chat with him. Time worked differently with children, and they might have felt that their father had been gone for ages rather than just a day. As she watched him with Kitty and Pierce, she could see both of them chattering away and looking up at him with absolute adoration. There was clearly much to say, and he was doing his best to give both of them adequate attention.

"They do love him so very much," Lady Downing said in a soft voice, her affection plain.

Cheeks heating, feeling rather caught, Rose shifted her eyes to Webb's mother quickly. "I can see that. Has it been a particularly eventful time while he's been at Fairview?"

"Not really," she replied, laughing to herself. "But they still want to tell him absolutely everything. And they've worked so very hard on gifts for him."

They passed the cemetery then, and Rose noticed that all of the adults lowered their heads respectfully. They did not stop speaking, if they were doing so, but their eyes were cast down and their manner subdued. Once they had moved beyond it, volume and energy resumed among the group.

Rose glanced behind them briefly, then ventured to ask, "Is Webb's wife buried there?"

Lady Downing nodded, her smile turning sad. "She is. Sweet Mary, she was like a daughter to me long before she married Webb. And the children will likely not remember her at all. That breaks my heart, but they have recovered so well after her death. Webb has given them so much devotion and attention, and Emily and the boys fill in so beautifully. I don't know how they would have managed without them."

"And what of Webb?" Rose inquired hesitantly. "Who took care of him while he took care of the children?"

"All of us," his mother told her. "And likely none of us. You know him a little—do you really think he would tell us how he was hurting or if he needed something in particular? He grieved, certainly, and it was some time before his smile reached his eyes once more. He rarely left Downing House, except for business, and even then, those trips were swift. It is only now that he has returned to social engagement for the sake of it."

Rose didn't know what to say to that. She had heard something of this from Webb himself upon their first meeting, but she hadn't expected so much of a retreat on his part. It sounded as though he had become almost a complete recluse in the wake of his wife's death, and that made her heart positively ache.

Her eyes began to burn with tears on his behalf, but she cleared them quickly with a cough. "You mentioned tiring out the children. Have they been particularly energetic this morning?"

"Oh heavens, yes." Lady Downing bounced Susan a little, smiling at the girl. "Even this one. She feeds on the energy of the others, and they are desperate for the gifts they will receive and the gifts they have to give. I hope you do not mind, but it would be best if we do the gifts before our meal, so it is out of the way."

"Not at all!" Rose reached out and ran a finger over Susan's arm gently, which made the girl smile. "Christmas presents are a delight."

They walked along the well-worn path away from the church and the village for a while, eventually turning upwards with the landscape and among thick patches of evergreen trees that lined the route. The air became heavy with the scent of pine, which was one of Rose's favorite smells in the world. It was a delightful addition to the day, and as they were walking towards the celebration of Christmas, pine was simply perfect.

The path turned at a break in the trees and suddenly Downing House was before them, at a different aspect from when Rose had arrived with Webb the other day, and yet it was no less stirring. There was just something about this house, its appearance, its setting among the grounds, that she adored, more than the grandeur of Fairview and the elegance of other fine houses. Downing was certainly elegant and grand in its own right, but it was understated and simplified. Or refined, perhaps.

That was it. A refined elegance and grandeur that begged to be properly appreciated.

The group entered the house and removed hats, bonnets, cloaks, and gloves, the children immediately darting for the stairs and racing up. Even Susan and Dominic demanded to be lowered to the ground so they could follow the others unaided. They were, of course, a trifle slower than the rest, but the adults did not mind the reduced pace of ascending the stairs.

Rose slowed her step as they followed the children into the same drawing room they'd been in before, wanting to allow the Rixton family members precedence to their own Christmas gathering. She hung back while the children darted here and there with their small presents for all of the adults, smiling at the reactions of everyone. Molly was quite proud of the bookmarks she was giving to everyone, which had ribbon carefully woven through lace. Her governess had helped her start each, she explained, but she had woven the ribbon all on her own.

Dominic and Susan did not seem to have any presents to bestow, but enjoyed running back and forth anyway. Kitty and Pierce were a pair, offering quills and pen wipers for their uncles, music for their aunt, and a small book of poetry for their grandmother. Then all of the other children waited and watched while Kitty and Pierce took a larger present to their father.

Webb seemed genuinely surprised about it and knelt before his children to open it. A pair of comfortable-looking slippers appeared from the brown paper, and Kitty squealed and clapped her hands when she saw them. It wasn't clear if she had forgotten that was the gift or if she was simply excited about it, but it was the most adorable reaction Rose had ever seen.

But then she looked at Webb. He was speechless as he looked at the slippers, then pulled both of his children into his arms, hugging them tightly. He kissed both and thanked them, his eyes appearing damp even from where Rose stood.

She quickly adjusted her opinion. *That* was the most adorable reaction she had ever seen.

Just when Rose thought the adults would start giving gifts to the children, Molly was running around again, this time with bits of greenery for everyone. It appeared she—with some help from capable adults—had arranged boutonnieres for the men and hair pieces for the women. Sprigs of holly or rosemary or hawthorn, or combinations of the sort, were now dotting buttonholes and carefully set hair. It was as entertaining as it was sweet, and Rose smiled as Emily and her mother helped each other fix the greenery into their hair.

Then, to Rose's astonishment, Molly and Kitty came over to her, their smiles nearly identical, showing the family resemblance quite plainly.

"Miss Rose," Molly began, her hands behind her back, "we didn't make you bits for your hair like Mama and Grandmama."

"Oh, sweet girl, that is absolutely—"

"We did something else," Molly went on, completely overriding Rose's attempt to soothe her.

She looked at her cousin, her tongue making a quick appearance between grinning teeth, then she brought forth an unmistakable crown of sorts. Kitty helped her to hold it, and they thrust it out to Rose. Ivy made up most of the crown, but there were several small white flowers strewn throughout, the handiwork clearly not that of children, but something they were just as proud of.

Rose put a hand to her heart and stooped to their height. "Oh, girls... That's so lovely!"

"They're Christmas roses," Molly explained, her voice practically squealing now.

"Like your name," Kitty added. She pointed at Rose for emphasis, her smile as sweet as her words.

Rose looked around at the adults, all of whom were watching the scene with varying expressions ranging from surprise to pride to delight. Webb was grinning as though this was the best Christmas ever, and he winked at Rose when their eyes met.

The lump in her throat responded in kind, cueing her eyes to water as she returned her attention to the girls. "It is the sweetest gift I have ever, ever received," she told them in all honesty. "Will you put it on my head for me?"

Both girls giggled and moved to settle the crown on her head, needing a bit of help from Emily to make it steady. Once it was set, Rose took the girls in her arms for a hug to resounding applause from the family.

"Who wants presents from Uncle Fred?" Fred bellowed, breaking the moment and blessedly taking attention away from Rose.

The girls dashed away and Rose wiped at her eyes, rising from the ground with a faint sniff.

Webb was at her side in an instant, though she hadn't seen him move. "I had no idea they were doing that," he murmured low, putting his arm around her shoulders in a sort of hug.

"I wish I had something to give them in return," Rose whispered, swallowing a faint hiccup of emotion.

His arm tightened around her, filling her body with light. "You're here. That is gift enough." He kissed her head, startling her, and then strode away to help Kitty open her present from Fred.

Rose watched him go, feeling her heart pounding hard with at least seven different emotions, none of which were willing to take the lead at being identified. Her eyes felt wide and rapidly drying, and her lips spread into a smile she did not comprehend nor intend. Nothing was making sense to her mind or in her body.

Nothing.

But it was Christmas Day and there was so much love in this room, she simply could not be bothered to untangle her feelings now. There would be time for that later.

Straightening her crown a little, Rose moved forward and sat down on one of the sofas to watch the children receive their gifts, reacting appropriately and enthusiastically for each.

CHAPTER 16

In future, Webb was not going to advise taking in two Christmas feasts in one day. It was delicious, but so markedly uncomfortable that he had no idea how he would be expected to dance after. He would much rather go for an extensive walk, even in the dark, and perhaps go to sleep. He wasn't particular about where he went to sleep; indoors on a bed would be lovely, but outside under the stars in the garden would also do.

But if it meant he could sit by Rose at a meal twice in one day, he just might repeat the experience.

It all depended on what happened after this meal was over.

The feast at Fairview was far grander than what they'd had at Downing a few hours ago, but that had been a meal designed to sate the appetites of children as well as adults, so the menu had been restricted. Here, on the other hand, there were quite as many vegetables as there were anything else, and at least seven different cuts of meats. Venison and goose, naturally, but there was also roast beef, capon, duck, pheasant, and pork, all steaming and well seasoned, according to the fragrances wafting through the entire room. From his present vantage point, Webb could also see brussels sprouts, potatoes, carrots, and squash, not to mention the stuffings for each of the fowls. Then there were mincemeat pies, plum puddings, fig pudding, five different kinds of bread, and black butter or any choice of preserves for that bread.

Webb was halfway through his meal and already wishing it were over. They hadn't even reached the Christmas pudding, and he was certain there would also be syllabubs, gingerbread, and marzipan. He'd already had one glass of mulled wine and was afraid to finish the second, but other guests were not so restrained.

The volume of conversation alone told him that a few of the gentlemen had chosen brandy instead of the mulled wine or claret, and some of the ladies were clearly indulging in more wine than they normally would.

"Tell me, Rose," Webb muttered, leaning closer to her on his left, "has the general party grown a bit merrier as the meal has gone on?"

She snickered around a bite of potato and nodded at once. "It has," she concurred after swallowing. "I think Lady Standhope has enhanced her beverages in the hopes that it might be a very merry Christmas evening."

"And she expects us to dance and perform music afterwards?" Webb shook his head slowly. "I shall need a long walk or a lie down before I can endure either of those things."

"What do you think I did when we returned from Downing?" Rose hissed back through a smile. "And, if you would care to notice, I am eating very delicate amounts." She took a particularly small bite of vegetable as though to prove her point.

Webb gave her a sardonic look. "No one will give you a sideways look for having a delicate appetite. I, on the other hand, will be asked if I require the care of a physician."

Rose shrugged, completely unconcerned. "There are some advantages to being a woman, I will concede."

Her little smile made him laugh as much as it nearly undid

151

him. She'd been wearing it practically all day, and he wished with all his might that she were still wearing the crown that Molly and Kitty had arranged for her. She'd obediently worn it the entire time she had been at the house, just as the rest of them had worn their bits of greenery, and he was not the only one who had seen it more as a halo than a crown. Bash had referred to her as an angel of Christmas at one point during the meal, though Webb thought the comment might have just been for him, and Emily had pointed out how well she looked with the hellebore flowers in full bloom against the sable darkness of her hair.

His eyes tracked over her hair now, willing the memory of those flowers and ivy to come to life, just for a moment. Then he started slightly, seeing two small white flowers tucked into the delicate chignon she wore now. One might miss them with the decorative pins scattered about, but he saw them, and the closer he looked, the more he was certain they were fresh flowers and not paper ones.

"Are you wearing some of your Christmas roses in your hair?" he asked hoarsely, wishing he'd been able to remove any and all emotion from the question. It could have been a teasing point, but alas…

Rose's cutlery clattered just a little. "Yes. Don't tell the girls I plucked these from the crown, I couldn't bear to break their hearts. I just wanted to keep wearing something of it for the rest of the day. Silly, really, but they were so sweet, and it *is* Christmas…"

Webb met her eyes, barely able to breathe. "It's perfect," he assured her, still not managing a steady voice. "Utterly perfect."

Her cheeks turned a slight shade of pink, and that small smile of hers quirked just a bit further, driving him absolutely mad. "It does add a little something to the ensemble, does it not?"

Considering Rose looked positively radiant in her gown of white and gold and green, he was not in a position to believe anything needed to be added to make her more beautiful or more perfect at this moment.

And yet, the flowers from his daughter and his niece, tucked into her hair when no one present but him would know the significance...

That *was* more perfect.

He did not need Rose to be more perfect. She needed to be less perfect. Far, far less. Otherwise he was going to be in very great danger in a very short time.

He hadn't been in that sort of danger for years.

God help him, he wanted that danger with her.

He nodded at her playful question, very belatedly, and returned his attention to his meal. "Do you know who you'll want to dance with this evening? Should the dancing be so structured, of course. It could all be rather haphazard."

"If everyone is this merry, yes, rather haphazard, indeed." Rose scoffed a little, taking a dainty sip of her wine. "It would tell me a great deal about the gentlemen, though. I could never marry a drunkard."

"I don't think any are here," Webb pointed out, willing his face to cool as he continued to eat. "Only those who occasionally overindulge. And it is a rare sort who never overindulges."

"Do you?"

Now why would she be asking him that question? And why the devil would she ask it at this moment?

"No," he said carefully around a bit of beef. "But my brothers do. Does Richard?"

Rose cocked her head at that. "Do you know, I have no idea? I've never seen Richard do so, but I cannot speak for him all the time, can I? I cannot see Alden or Colin doing so either, they are far too practical for that. But Alexander absolutely would, probably any given Thursday..."

Webb let Rose go on, listing as many of her male relations

and associates as she liked and her views on whether they drank to excess, as it gave him more time to gather his wits and his thoughts, if not further his completion of his meal. Without this time to do so, he might find himself drinking to excess just to try and feel less desperate about his present state of existence.

This could not be what his sister and mother had envisioned by his attending this party. Not this sudden madness rapidly becoming an obsession. Nobody wanted their relation turned into that sort of creature, and Webb had prided himself on always being sensible even when he was sociable. Especially when he was sociable. He was reasonable, predictable, and reliable.

Always able.

He was not very able now. He was rather unable to understand himself, and that was maddening.

Still, the mulled wine could be clouding his thoughts, so he might find more clarity in the morning along with a decent headache, which might cure everything. There was nothing like a headache to ground one in reality, even if it was miserable.

"Pierce was so delighted to find a shilling in his pudding," Rose said with a laugh, breaking into Webb's self-absorbed thoughts. "I don't believe I've ever seen a child so enthusiastic about a surprise bite."

Webb smiled at that, remembering his son's shrieks of delight earlier in the day. "I know. One would think he'd never seen money before. I think I will wait to tell him how much a farthing is worth."

"Especially with Dominic getting a half a crown," Rose pointed out with a tilt of her head. "And Molly a sovereign. But at least Kitty and Susan only managed pennies each. Odd how none of the adults managed money…"

"Odd, indeed." Webb smirked and shrugged a little. "What can I say? The children must be lucky."

Rose nodded in approval. "Do you know, I believe they are.

Your children—and your nieces and nephew—are very lucky. Perhaps the most fortunate children I know." She sobered a little, her smile rather gentle. "They know how loved they are, they know they can be their silly selves, and they know that any of the adults in their lives will take care of them. I call that incredibly fortunate. Not all families are so indulgent."

Webb glanced at her more closely, knowing he was staring and others might see, but feeling a prickle of concern starting to tease at his ears and his stomach. "Rose?"

She shook herself a little and smiled more fully, and he saw that it did reach her eyes, much to his relief. "I am not speaking of myself, Webb. Not really. I may have had to pretend for my mother a few times out in Society, but my family is very loving. They show it in different ways than yours—"

"That's not surprising," he said with a snort. "We're an unusual bunch."

"But," Rose went on, laughing lightly, "I never wished my family would be different. Well, I might have wished that my sisters would frown more so I would not feel so different, but that is not a fault of theirs. Rather my own, I think."

"It is not a fault to have a range of emotions," Webb insisted dryly, resuming his eating with a halfhearted effort. "I am fairly certain that is the way human existence is meant to be, but no one has ever instructed me on the exact details of the subject. If it makes you feel any better, it is likely one or more of your sisters might explode with pent-up emotions in the future."

Rose choked on her wine, which made Webb snicker in delight. She picked up her napkin and dabbed at her mouth in the most delicate manner possible, her shoulders trembling with unshed laughter.

"You wretch," she hissed in a tight voice. "Don't do that!"

"Do what?" he asked mildly, taking a bite of his black-butter-laden bread. "I was simply saying..." He had to pause as she continued to laugh, her napkin going back to her mouth. "Now I have to know which sister you are imagining exploding and how that would go," he added in a much lower voice. "In great detail."

"Marina," Rose answered at once, a hand going to her throat as she tried to calm herself. "She is the most effervescent of my sisters. She looks the most like me, though her hair is paler and closer to a dirty-golden color. She would be the one to go first." She made a sound between a laugh and a snort, closing her eyes for a moment. "This is terrible, Webb."

Again, he shrugged, this time rather pointedly. "I'm enjoying it. Exploding sisters ought to be something discussed with more frequency. Emily explodes all the time, but she's not as constantly cheery as your sisters, from the sound of things. I blame Fred and Bash. I am sure they've provoked her enough to give her quite the range of emotions."

"But never you?" Rose inquired with a mild raise of her brow.

Shaking his head with solemn firmness, Webb forced his expression into one of pure innocence. "I was the most responsible elder brother. Always respectful, always caring, always ensuring her protection. I told you yesterday, I kept her from falling down the stairs due to her blasted skirts several times."

Rose clamped down on her lips, her mouth trying to stretch into a grin at the same time. "Quite the hero, aren't you?"

If she hadn't said it with the utmost sarcasm and dryness, he might have been flattered and become a trifle overcome again. As it was, he was far more entertained and delighted that she was bantering with him. That she seemed to enjoy bantering with him as much as he did her. That they had this beautiful, strange, entertaining connection between them that was so rooted in a shared sense of humor.

It was just as enjoyable as her moments of genuine compliments and flattering honesty, if he were to admit the truth. "I do try," Webb allowed with an indulgent nod. The desserts came out then, and he almost groaned at the impending discomfort. The jellies, syllabubs, fruit tarts, and pastries all looked positively divine, but how in the world was he meant to function after this?

"You look more pained than a gentleman dancing a fourth quadrille in a row," Rose told him with a laugh.

"I may need four quadrilles in a row to maintain any sort of physique after eating this," he said, making a face. "Lord knows when I'll be able to physically manage a single quadrille, nevertheless...needs must." He exhaled dramatically as he looked at the dish of syllabub placed before him.

Rose giggled as she picked up her spoon, readying to eat her own. "You mustn't offend our hostess."

"It is true," he concurred. "I must not." With a grin he usually reserved for impish antics with his siblings, he quirked his brows and took a heaping bite of syllabub, sighing with pleasure at its taste.

The entire table enjoyed the desserts, as evidenced by the plethora of sounds of appreciation resounding throughout the room. One look at Lady Standhope told Webb that she took each and every one as a personal victory, if not personal compliment. Given the sheer volume of people in attendance at this house party, Webb could not blame her.

Then again, would anyone actually admit if they were *not* enjoying her food?

It was not too long before they were all invited to leave the dining room and move into the music room, which had been arranged in such a way that dancing could take place, but also that people could sit in chairs for a concert. Webb doubted that dancing would happen while people were singing, but the chairs would certainly be most welcome for those who were not going to dance at all. He did note that the music room was adjacent to the terrace, which had stairs down to the garden and the grounds, so perhaps a walk would be something he could do. He would certainly enjoy the cool night air after the feasts of the day, and he was feeling an exceptional amount of gratitude for the people and the goodness in his life.

Such feelings would be better suited to solitude and the openness of the outdoors. The stars in the sky and the leaves of hedges being the only witnesses. The only conversation that of the breeze against one's hair and cheeks.

He needed such an escape.

Lady Standhope rang a small bell at the front of the music room, startling Webb out of his focus on the terrace. "Ladies and gentlemen, I think we are all a bit befuddled by the meal, so perhaps we might enjoy a few songs from our guests before we begin any dancing. Unless someone is feeling particularly light."

A round of good-natured laughter came from the group, and Webb smiled at it.

"Could we have a waltz, Lady Standhope?" one of the young ladies asked brightly. "Before any performances, I mean. I desperately want to waltz at the moment."

There was more laughter, louder this time, even from Lady Standhope. Webb wondered if the young lady was slightly under the influence of the evening's wine to admit such a bold thing.

"Oh, why not?" Lady Standhope set her bell on the pianoforte and beamed. "Mrs. Fellowes, would you play a waltz for us?"

Mrs. Fellowes agreed at once and went to the instrument. Several guests moved to the area set aside for dancing, but Webb remained where he was, content to observe and listen for the time being.

A soft hissing sound came from his right and he turned in

surprise. Rose stood there, the picture of absolute loveliness, her cheeks tinged with an enchanting shade of pink.

"Yes?" he greeted with a teasing air, trying to hide his curiosity.

She tilted her head towards the dancing, lips twisting a little. "To claim participation, should anyone ask."

Webb blinked at her, his smile frozen on his face. "Are you asking me to waltz?"

"No," Rose said with a laugh. "I am suggesting that you ask me to waltz so we might both safely say we were active participants in the activities of Christmas Day. You know there are some who will ask us both. Lying is a sin, after all."

He didn't care if lying were a new breed of flower, the color of the sky, or the name of the next great inventor. All he knew was that Rose wanted to waltz with him, and any excuse to do so was the best one he'd ever heard in his entire life. Stuffed with excellent food or not, he was going to waltz with her even if it were the slowest and most immobile waltz known to man. He'd have waltzed with her on one leg, if necessary.

She probably would not have made the suggestion to waltz if he had only one leg, but he'd have done it anyway.

"A sin," Webb repeated dazedly, thinking more of a sin would have been to refuse her than anything else. "Yes, of course." He held out his hand and she took it without hesitation, allowing him to lead her to the other couples.

It had never occurred to him to curse the wearing of gloves, but that was all his mind was doing at the present. Cursing their texture, the thickness of their fabric, and their very existence, as it kept him from feeling Rose's palm against his own. It would keep him from doing so the entire dance, and nothing had ever chafed quite like his own gloves against his hands at this very moment.

With a swallow that seemed to contain his entire life in its lump, Webb steered Rose into the already waltzing couples, locking his eyes with hers once they were securely in the formation.

He lost sense of everything else once he'd done so. How was it possible to view the entire essence of a person simply through their eyes? How could he see the beauty of sharing Christmas Day with her, the amusement of introducing her to his siblings, the very first moment they'd met, all at once? How could her eyes never be quite the same shade from one moment to the next, but always be exquisite? How was she capable of making every moment of his day seem to matter more than the one before?

More to the point, how was he even moving in this dance while he was so connected with her? He felt his pulse in his hands, his head, his chest, his ears, and for whatever reason, his knees, and it was keeping perfect time with the music and the pace of the waltz itself. He had no idea what her pulse was doing; his own was overwhelming everything, and he knew instinctively that it would not do the same for any other woman.

There was just Rose.

Only Rose.

Her smile was particularly beguiling at the moment, something between a laugh and a sigh, her lips appearing full and rosy. If he kissed her now, would she taste of wine? Of syllabub? Fruit? Would there be some honey to her kiss that brought him to his knees and ended his life as he knew it?

He dragged his eyes away from her mouth, knowing such focus would not only be noticed, but potentially disrupt the dance between them, which would almost certainly kill him.

Rose's eyes were darker now, bordering on a shade of violet, and his stomach clenched so hard, his breath was ripped from him.

What was she feeling? What was she thinking? Could she possibly be aware of how much she consumed his thoughts? How much he hated the idea of pairing her with anyone at this house party? Or in the entire world?

How torn he felt about her aunt Edith, giving him both the opportunity to meet Rose and the cause to lose her?

He did not even have her, but as her friend...

Her friend...

He did not want to be her friend anymore. Of course, he loved their friendship and valued it, but he wanted to add to it. Add so much more and let the beauty of that unfold before them.

Such a realization did nothing for his state of breathing nor the pace of his pulse, which skittered off the pace of the dance for a few beats.

Her fingers twitched in his hold. What did that mean? What had she felt? What did she think about this dance with him?

What did she think about him?

Then the waltz was over, and Webb was releasing his hold on her waist, keeping her hand in his a moment more.

"Thank you," Rose murmured, her voice not quite as steady as her steps had been.

Blessed day, he'd never loved a tremble in words more in his life.

"Of course," he rasped, unable to do more. He swallowed again. "Will you dance more later? With your list?"

Rose kept her eyes on his, then shook her head slowly. "I don't think so. I am done for the night."

Webb wanted to beam at the admission, but his mouth refused to cooperate, thankfully. He nodded and led her to a seat, but did not sit himself.

"Are you not going to listen to the music?" she asked.

"No," he said shortly, finally managing a smile. "I find I am in need of a walk in the night air. Excuse me." He nodded, kissed her glove, and turned on his heel for the terrace, craving the cool night air and the calm that would—hopefully—accompany it.

CHAPTER 17

Was it in terribly poor taste for Rose to be at the Rixton family fox hunt on St. Stephen's Day instead of the one at Fairview? No one had quite explained the rules of a house party to her in such matters, but she did not believe she would enjoy following a hunt of that many men. The Rixton party would boast less than a dozen involved in the hunt, including women following, and she liked those individuals involved a great deal more in general.

And a few in particular.

After her dance with Webb last night, she'd been more conflicted than ever before on any subject or person in her life. Breathless as well as exhilarated, replete from the experience and craving more of the same, wanting nothing more than to spend the rest of the night in his company even if they said nothing at all. And then he had said he needed to walk in the night air and left her to listen to the music on her own.

Not before kissing her hand, which had sent fire directly to her heart, but he had left her all the same.

And then she had not seen him for the rest of the night. And without Webb beside her, joining her in an unnecessary commentary that would have them both snickering, all of the music, and enjoyment of it, had paled a little compared to what it could have been.

Finding a note slipped beneath her door this morning inviting her to join the fox hunt at Downing House had immediately lifted the spirits that had been low from the night before. Everything from the neat slanting of the words to the perfect "W" signing at the bottom of the note had her skipping about her room and flinging herself on her bed, just as she had done upon her arrival at Fairview. Now she was in her one good riding habit, praying it suited her, and had Emily beside her for company while the men were up ahead as part of the hunt.

"I am so relieved you came," Emily told her now as they rode along. "Bertram told me he wasn't certain if any other women were going to come, and my brothers would have howled about tradition and my role as their sister if I hadn't gone."

Rose smiled easily at that. "Is it really so dreadful?"

"With proper company, no." Emily laughed at once. "Alone? Psht." She shook her head and rolled her eyes dramatically. "I have done that once, and I never will again. Would you believe that three grown men are willing to make a great show of themselves just to impress their sister? Their sister, Rose. The person who likely cares less about most of the things they do than anyone else."

"Even Webb?" Rose asked, having some significant doubts about that.

Still, Emily nodded, her chin very firm in its motion. "He'd never do it on his own, and possibly not even if only one of the boys were with him, but when they are both here? He becomes a more stupid version of himself, far more competitive and reckless, even if it is still not as wild as what Fred and Bash get up to. They bring that out in him, and it's both hilarious and ridiculous at once."

Rose considered that, even between laughter at imagining it. "I suppose I can understand that. I become a lighter version of myself when I am with my sisters. It is mostly pretend, as I am trying to match them in some way, but not entirely. Their combined positivity, which grates on me most of the time, is somehow contagious anyway." She shrugged a little, now laughing at herself. "It is certainly contagious with their children. They all smile and laugh near constantly."

"That'll change," Emily assured her quickly. "And I am certain they are on best behavior in your company."

"True enough, I suppose." Rose inhaled deeply, loving the scent of nature on a brisk day and the freshness that filled her lungs with every breath. And the grounds at Downing were even more wonderful than she'd anticipated from what she'd seen so far. How did one spend any time indoors living in a place like this?

"Are you all right?" Emily asked with some concern when Rose exhaled on a long sigh. "That seemed particularly heavy."

Rose tossed her head back, laughing merrily. "Yes! I was just relishing the air of being out in nature, and among these grounds... My sisters adore London, so my parents almost never go home to Derbyshire, which means I do not get to go home to Derbyshire. The country is just exhilarating, and were we not on this hunt, I would beg to ride hard across the grounds just for the pleasure of it."

"You and Webb," Emily murmured, shaking her head even as her mouth curved in a smile.

The breath in Rose's lungs disintegrated at once, threatening to collapse those lungs in an instant.

"Wh-what about us?" she inquired with a light laugh she did not feel a jot.

"Oh, you are simply very similar in that regard." Emily looked ahead towards the men, a fond smile on her lips.

Relief hit Rose in waves, and she did her best to look attentive without showing any of that relief on her face.

"Webb has always been the best rider of any of us," Emily went on, straightening in her saddle, "but more than that, he is the one with the most interest in the country and this estate. It is fortunate that he is the eldest and thus inherited the estate and title, since none of us could possibly love this place more than he does."

Rose couldn't help it, she looked at the men ahead of them and picked out Webb from among them, even through the coats and hats. She couldn't study his riding from this vantage point, but she imagined him as the most capable rider, the most relaxed in this situation, the one who might inhale the air just as she had done. The sudden image of racing against him across these gorgeous hills and stretches of green, both of them pushing hard on their horses, hair whipping wildly about them, laughing just as recklessly on the wind...

She wasn't in her riding habit in this race, just an average day dress, and free of a bonnet. Webb wasn't in a jacket and hat on this ride, he was in a linen shirt with sleeves rolled to the elbows, looking years younger without the formal clothing to accompany him. It was the most attractive picture of him she had ever seen, and it only existed in her mind.

Why? Why was that an image her imagination had conjured up and why did she positively ache for it? It was as though her soul was keening for it, taking her heart in hand and steering it hard in whatever direction might bring it out. She had to stop herself from rubbing at her chest, a physical twinge of the aching making itself known.

"But then, Webb loves everything fiercely."

Rose jerked to a more perfect posture at these words, her throat clenching. "Everything?" she repeated, somehow finding a laugh at her disposal. "He does not love charades, ghost stories, or excessive eating, I can tell you that much."

Emily laughed as well and gave Rose a quick grin. "That is not what I mean! Goodness sakes, can you imagine someone who actually loves every single thing?"

"I have sisters who seem to," she grumbled, relieved that they could possibly move off the subject of Webb until she was more settled. "Harriet in particular."

"She loves everything?" Emily looked rather dubious at the claim. "I doubt that very much."

"Perhaps not, but she acts like it." Rose took a moment to look at the trees in the distance, collecting her thoughts. "Harriet does not like to express a contrary opinion. She thinks it makes her disagreeable, and the last time she was disagreeable, in her eyes, she worried about it so much that she broke out in a rash."

Rose rolled her eyes at this, as it had all been very dramatic for Harriet, but all had cleared within a matter of hours and there had been no lasting harm to anyone. Her sister had been all but fifteen at the time, but Rose, for one, had not seen her frown since.

At all.

"She was perfectly well," Rose went on, realizing that she needed to complete the story adequately. "But it seems to have forced her into believing that anything other than being content at all times will make her ill, or some such. She will only express an opinion if it is the majority, such as my coming to this house party at Fairview and bringing a maid with me."

"You did not want to come initially?" Emily inquired with a sympathetic click of her tongue.

How much had Webb told his sister? Did she know anything about Rose's situation and what had prompted her to come to Fairview at all? What would Emily make of the scheme, if she learned of it? Could a woman as happily married and situated as Emily possibly understand Rose's motivation for it? And beyond that, what would she make of Webb's involvement?

"Not really," she eventually admitted with a sheepish smile. "It was my aunt's idea for me to come. She believes I need to marry and wanted me to find someone at this house party to wed. If I did that, she would grant me a quiet cottage in the countryside, and a stipend to keep it up. Knowing how I have always wanted a quiet country living, she knew I would be tempted into action by the prospect."

There, she had just admitted what exactly had brought her here. Let her think of it what she would and make whatever assumptions she would.

Emily was staring at her with a confused expression, faint creases between her brows. "If you find someone to marry...at this house party...you can go off and live quietly in a cottage? What is the point of a marriage if you are going to live on your own in solitude?"

Rose burst out laughing, loving that Emily's mind went in that direction rather than something critical of Rose or Webb.

"I am in earnest!" Emily insisted, not laughing nearly as much as Rose, but finding some amusement in her reaction. "Take it from a happily married wife, Rose: There are easier ways to exist. What does she want you to be married for? Independence? Security?"

"She says love," Rose confided before she could stop herself. "But she also believes I am difficult and prickly, so I am beginning to think she has set me on a course to prove a point. If I were in love, why would I want to live alone in her offered cottage? She specifically forbade a marriage of convenience, which would make far more sense. So either she wishes me to have a broken heart, or she has no intention of giving me the cottage."

Emily exhaled in an irritated burst of air. "I have so many questions for this aunt of yours."

"That's almost exactly what Webb said, if I recall." Rose smiled. "I had been thinking of asking someone to marry me and simply act as though it were a love match to satisfy my aunt."

"I can understand that reasoning, certainly." Emily nodded in approval, then stopped. "Would it be dreadful if we waited to see how far they get before following at pace?"

"I don't think so, no," Rose quipped.

They shared a quick smile, not encouraging their horses in the slightest.

But talking of Webb, even a little, and imagining him riding, had brought Rose's mind back to something his sister had said before, and she could not let go of it.

"Emily," she began carefully, "what *did* you mean when you said that Webb loves everything fiercely?"

Emily glanced over at her, the faint crease appearing between her brows again. "Oh, that was just a sister exaggerating about her brother. Don't mind me."

It was an obvious attempt to minimize the subject, but Rose couldn't let it go. "Please," she said softly.

Emily watched her for a long moment, then sighed. "Webb is… intense, I suppose, in the way he loves and cares. What he loves, he loves with everything he is. I have no doubt that if I were ever in trouble, either in my marriage or financially, Webb would move heaven and earth to save me somehow. There is a great beauty in that, but it also means that I take great care in what I tell him. My marriage is not in danger, and I have no financial problems—those were just examples, you understand."

Rose nodded quickly, hoping Emily would continue to enlighten her.

"After Mary died," she went on, "Webb threw himself into the lives of his children. He had always been an active, engaging, loving father, but he suddenly became consumed by his role. He turned his grieving into excessive attention for them, as though he needed to become mother and father in one so they would not feel any loss at all. I have no way of knowing how he grieved in private, I can only speak to what I saw, but we were all quite concerned. He refused to be apart from his children because they would miss him. I think the truth of it was that he would miss them, and he was too afraid of losing something else he loved."

A faint burning began in Rose's eyes, and her throat constricted a few times, trying to force a swallow. She could almost picture the desperation in Webb that Emily was describing, his face constantly etched with concern that he prayed his children wouldn't see. He would have done everything in his power, if not beyond it, to make his children smile and be happy just to spare them the hurt and the tears.

She began to hurt again, deep within her soul, for the man riding far ahead of them. For the loss he had endured and the losses he feared, for the grief that altered him, for the depth of his pain...

"Everything is fierce and intense for Webb," Emily told Rose, looking at her quite steadily now. "Nothing is superficial. Genuine friendship, genuine concern, genuine anger, genuine love, and he does nothing halfway. It is a great blessing and probably also a curse, but it is the essence of Webb."

Sensing she was being advised, in a sense, Rose nodded very slowly. Whatever Emily wanted her to take from the information, she couldn't say, but she suspected it was a deeper insight than she might have received on her own.

And yet...she could feel that in Webb. His humor was always real and genuine, his consideration much the same, and his attentiveness to Rose at the house party showed a real dedication to their odd friendship in spite of the scheme that had brought her across his path.

Then there had been that waltz...

There had been so much—*so much*—in that single dance. So much that she had felt, but also so much that she had seen in Webb. Things that had confused her and excited her, things that frightened her and things that awakened her, and it created this bewildering battle of nothing in her life making sense and suddenly everything making sense as well.

She was rapidly losing interest in any sort of list or comfortable arrangement for her own independence. Would it be possible for her to simply enjoy the rest of the house party and her time with Webb? Ignore everything that Aunt Edith had promised her, relish every second she could with this man, and then go back to her father's original promise of her dowry at five-and-thirty? She would know herself so much better after this experience, and who knew what the future could bring?

It was impossible to ignore her feelings, but it was also impossible to identify them.

What did she want? That was the question that haunted her at the moment. She had spent so long wanting to be left alone, after years of regularly being forced into a long series of events that always ended in disappointments, that it had never occurred to her that anything else was possible. She had convinced herself that the only solution for her happiness was that escape she had clung to.

What if there was something else after all?

Somehow, Rose managed conversation with Emily during the rest of the ride, and they did eventually catch up with the gentlemen as they raced after the hounds. Even with the brisk galloping to do so, she felt only half-aware of her surroundings.

It was a quiet ride back to Downing House, and Rose could not be sorry for that. She needed time to think, and thinking would not best be done here. The family would have more to do as tenants and servants were gifted their annual measures, and Rose could return to Fairview and rejoin Lady Standhope's party. Or, more likely, hole up in the library and distract her mind away from complicated thoughts with a good book.

Webb, as host of the foxhunt, was up at the head of the

riders, his brothers and Bertram mingled among the group, and Emily had chosen to ride with them on the way back, no doubt to continue their bickering. She would bid them all farewell if needed, but it would be so much the better to slip away with the rest of the guests. If she were drawn into engagement with the full family again, she might never leave.

Ever.

And that was a terrifying thought. And a lovely thought. And one she could not presently contemplate.

There were just enough guests and riders at the foxhunt for her to dismount at the stables without any sort of fanfare or notice by the Rixtons. She awkwardly tied the skirts of her riding habit up behind her, then twirled her crop a little as she walked back to the house, her eyes on the ground before her, head beginning to ache with her swirling thoughts. The line of riders streamed steadily into the kitchen for warm drinks and a light repast, and given the majority of the servants were not working on this day, there would be plenty of room for them all.

Was it usual for riders and hunters to see the kitchen of such an estate? The very informal nature of it was refreshing to Rose, and likely comfortable for the guests who were of the poorer landed gentry or tenants, but it also seemed to be very much the air of the Rixton family and how they interacted with others. Plenty of familiarity, plenty of comfort, plenty of humility, and all warmth and openness.

The large kitchen boasted a roaring blaze in a large stone fireplace, and many of the riders were helping themselves to a bowl of steaming punch on a sturdy wooden table. The conversation was energetic and light, everyone cheery and laughing as befitted the Christmas season. It was impossible to be in the same space and not smile along with everyone else, and Rose was not even participating in any of the discussions.

She took note of the position of all four Rixton siblings and

Bertram, seeing each was actively engaged with their guests and neighbors. It would be presumptuous for her to intrude and call attention to herself, which she certainly did not wish to do, especially among strangers. They had things to do, and she did not want to interfere with them.

Without meeting any eyes, Rose ducked into the saloon beside the kitchen, making her way towards the front of the house, as far as she could tell. This seemed to be the way she had been led in that morning, but as she had not explored Downing House with the same thoroughness that she'd been afforded at Fairview, she could not be certain. Still, if she came across any servants or Lady Downing, she could always ask for directions.

Fortunately, the corridor off the saloon led directly to the anteroom and entrance hall of the ground floor, and Rose heaved a sigh of relief at seeing it.

Crosby, the family's butler, was there and seemed to be heading in the direction Rose had just come from. His eyes brightened as he saw her and he smiled quickly, pausing for a deep bow. "Miss Portman, is there something I might help you with?"

Rose returned his smile. "Yes, Crosby. I don't wish to trouble the family while they have so many friends and neighbors still about, and with the boxes to be distributed after. Would it be possible to have a carriage called to take me back to Fairview?"

"Of course, Miss Portman. I will see to it at once." He nodded firmly and continued on his way, disappearing from her sight in a moment.

She began to walk slowly around the space, looking at the sculptures, pillars, and sets of furniture on either side of it. The ceiling was adorned with some lovely plasterwork, almost brocade in style and touched with gold paint in some places. The paint was worn in other spots, clearly a factor of age and decay, but all of it still well-kept and clean. It was an oddly comforting sight, those imperfections.

Relatable, even.

"See anything delightful or fascinating up there?"

Rose's heart leapt and skipped at Webb's voice and she turned to face him, smiling entirely without intending to. "Quite. It's lovely artwork."

Webb strode easily towards her, looking practically boyish with his hair in slight disarray and still dressed in hunting attire. "I shall pass on the compliments, though I think the descendants of the artisans have stopped caring." His smile softened and his brows rose. "Were you going to leave without a word?"

"You were occupied," Rose murmured with a faint gesture towards the back of the house. "I didn't want to impose."

"It wouldn't have been an imposition. Surely you know that." He came over to her and, without warning, took a hand in hers. "You won't stay?"

Something burst with a startling heat right where Rose's heart lay, and she shook her head, her smile almost ticklish now. "No, I'll go back to Fairview. You have so much to do with your guests back there, and with the boxes later... I won't be any help with that, and you should really enjoy those traditions with your family. Perhaps Lady Standhope has something planned for her guests that I can take part in."

Webb laughed very softly, his thumb running over Rose's hand. She still had gloves on, but it was no matter. She could feel his touch like a combination of fire and ice, each pass of his thumb spiraling the sensation deeper and deeper into her skin. "You mean to tell me that you'll volunteer for her arrangements?"

"Well, it depends on what they are," Rose conceded with a wrinkle of her nose, allowing a faint laugh to escape. "There is always the library otherwise."

He nodded in response—either in understanding or approval, it was difficult to tell. Or perhaps it was just the feeling of his thumb distracting her from clarity of thought.

"It means a great deal that you came today, Rose," Webb told her, his voice lower than before as he stepped even closer. "I know we didn't talk or spend any time together, but…I am so glad you came."

"I enjoyed myself," she whispered, nodding for no apparent reason. "I love being here. I love this place. I love…" Her voice caught on whatever she was going to say next, wherever her words were going to tumble, and there was nothing left but the breath in her body and all that was unspoken.

Webb's eyes were dark and focused, intent on her, his lips holding just the slightest curve to them. Then he ran a finger of his free hand over her cheek, just the back of it smoothing over the chilled contour of her skin in the gentlest caress.

"I love you being here," he told her, the combination of words and touch making her shiver. "I love this place more when you're here."

"Don't t-tease me," Rose pleaded on a faint breath, her eyes fluttering.

Webb shook his head just once. "I'm not." Then his mouth was on hers, his finger sliding beneath her chin to tip her face up, closer to his own. The kiss was slow and grazing, the lightest caress of lips, less of hesitation and more of subtlety.

Rose, who had never been kissed before in her life, felt some guttural sound curling in her throat, mingling with a pant as her fingers gripped at the hand holding hers.

Something similar seemed to come from Webb, and his lips were on hers again. This time, she leaned into it, that sound sending power into the arches of her feet and raising her up. Webb cradled her face with one hand, the other never leaving hers, and his lips passed over hers with a thorough tenderness that seemed designed to unravel the entire fabric of her being thread by painstaking thread. She had never felt anything like this, as though light were filling her body and jolts of energy were screeching their way into her limbs. Her heart roared its beat into her ears, practically crashing from one pulse to the next like waves against steep cliffs. Crashing and rolling and colliding, breath and beats and an all-powerful burning from those lips all she cared about.

Webb pressed a final whisper-kiss against her cheek, his breathing unsteady against her skin. He nuzzled ever so slightly against her, releasing a rough, rumbling exhale.

"Mistletoe?" Rose breathed.

"Don't say anything, Rose," he whispered, his lips catching on her skin with the words. "Not a thing."

She felt him swallow, felt the pressure increase on her hand, and then he was gone, walking back towards the kitchen without looking back, his hands clenching and unclenching by his sides.

Rose stared after him, long after his back had disappeared and long after her trembling had stopped.

Webb loves everything fiercely.

Her throat clenched at the reminder of Emily's words. Whether that was what was taking place here or not, Rose was suddenly filled with more fear than she had ever felt in her entire life. She could not do this. Could not break his heart. Could not pretend that she was a match for him. Could not...

Could not.

Crosby appeared through the doorway and nodded at her. "The carriage is out front, Miss Portman. This way, please."

Rose tried to return his nod, glancing up at the ceiling and finding no mistletoe. With a gasp, she followed Crosby and gripped at her collar ever so slightly, wondering if it were possible for clothing to strangle the wearer in protest.

She needed the solitude of Fairview more than ever. She had to know her own mind before anything else happened.

She had to.

CHAPTER 18

Webb was going to tear Fairview apart if he went another day without speaking a word with Rose.

It had been four full days since their kiss at Downing, and she had not appeared at supper that night. She had not been exploring the house the next morning, nor any morning since. She'd not been in the library anytime he had checked, and all of his notes had gone unanswered. The only time he had seen her had been supper the last two nights, where she had sat to Lady Standhope's left and never appeared at the evening entertainment.

What excuses she was giving their hostess, he could not say, and he did not dare ask. Looking too eager would raise questions, and he did not want word of Rose's nonparticipation to reach her aunt Edith. If he had not seen her at those meals, he would have thought she had left Fairview entirely. It was a great relief to him that she had not. There was still a chance if she was still here.

There was so much Webb wanted to tell Rose. So much he wanted to ask. And if she continued to be absent, those questions would only grow. And change. And become more desperate.

If she bothered to look at any of the notes he had sent, Rose would know that he was not going to ask her any intimidating questions. Nothing too life-altering or noteworthy. He simply wanted to know if she had felt the same way as he did about their kiss. If she wanted to come with him to Downing for New Year's. If she would be his partner for whatever pairings were required on Twelfth Night.

Simple things, really.

The more terrifying question that lurked in the back of his mind—and it did lurk there—would hinge on how those questions were answered and how those occasions played out.

He would not presume anything. He knew better in general, and he certainly knew much better with Rose.

Rose was unlike any other woman he had ever met. She knew her mind with a startling clarity. She expressed her opinions with blistering honesty. She did exactly as she liked with frightening certainty.

So why was she avoiding him?

He'd given up searching for her during the day today and had gone back home to Downing for recuperation and a taste of some happiness. The children had been an able distraction for him, creating all sorts of imaginary games with the greenery still hung about the house. And when it was time for them all to rest in the nursery, Webb had sat with Emily for a time, saying nothing.

It was she, as it happened, who brought up the subject of Rose. And then he had started to talk. And talk. And talk. Unable to stop, it seemed, and saying far more than he should have and somehow never quite reaching a point. He unburdened his entire soul to his sister, which was likely not what she had intended, but it was highly overdue on his part.

How meeting Rose had been an accident in and of itself. How it had begun as a lark and an excuse to avoid anyone else. How it had become more and more entertaining every passing hour. How Rose had awakened something in him that he hadn't even known was dormant. How much brighter life appeared because of her. How he seemed to laugh more and wish to live more. There just seemed to be so much more of life because of and when he was with Rose.

He had known all of that since St. Stephen's Day, at the very least. He had been helpless against kissing her, all of the gloriousness of her person and her essence overwhelming him until he finally gave in to what he had been dreaming about for days. It had surpassed everything he had anticipated, and he'd been without words.

Which, ironically, was why he had insisted that Rose say nothing either. Words would have changed the moment, and he could not bear for it to alter a jot.

Except now he had no other moments, romantic or entertaining, to add to it, so there were no words at all for what had happened.

No laughter, no shared looks, no anything.

It could not end that way.

Emily had not given him much by way of advice, but she did relay something she had told Rose during their ride.

"I told her you love everything fiercely," Emily had admitted. "Whatever you love, you love it with everything you are."

He couldn't argue the point. He had always felt his emotions intensely, and he did not know any other way to live his life. Surely that hadn't been what Rose was hiding from. He hadn't told her he loved her, after all.

Granted, he *did* love her, and he'd finally admitted that to himself as he'd ridden gloomily back to Fairview. It was such a different love from what he'd felt for Mary. Not more intense or deeper or in any way better or worse—just different. The relationship they'd had was so longstanding and the feelings had grown so naturally and progressively that it had simply become part of who he was.

With Rose, everything was full of surprises. It rolled and shifted and changed, rather like the landscape of Yorkshire itself. It was wild and captivating and regularly left him breathless. Falling in love with Rose was like a whirlwind he'd been caught up in, and now he felt the silence and the calm in such a hollow, lifeless manner.

He needed her in his life. He needed the brightness she brought and the laughter she'd restored. But if she wouldn't see him, how could any of that come about?

What had frightened her? Or disgusted her? What had he done that meant she could not face him? Or be his friend, at least. Whatever else they might have been, or were becoming, they were friends, were they not? Allies? If she had decided something about him and about them, perhaps in favor of the list and her aunt's plan, he would still try to help her. It might kill him, but he was a man of his word, and above all else, he wanted Rose to be happy with the life that was before her.

Did he love her enough to let her marry someone else because she chose to?

Possibly, but he would not be able to attend the ceremony.

He could not endure the rest of the house party like this, that much was plain. He needed to see her again and encourage her to be as frank and honest as she had ever been. Tell him exactly what she felt and what she wanted and how she wanted them to proceed. There was nothing worse than a one-sided romance, he was certain, but a one-sided romance because one was ignorant of the other side was pure torment.

Hope was a torment. If he knew there was no hope, at least he could move on and try to pick up the pieces of his life and his heart.

At least he would know that he had a heart once more.

Webb closed the book he had been pretending to read in the library with a sharp snap, rising from his chair and replacing it on the shelf he'd plucked it from. He did not acknowledge any of the others in the room, though there were only three, and instead left entirely, moving down the corridor without a specific destination in mind. Perhaps he would go outside. A ride would be just the thing to make time pass in an enjoyable way and perhaps give him enough of a change to create some decent ideas.

But he would need to change for the sort of ride he wanted to take. This was no time for polite trotting and caution. He wanted to go for a hard, reckless ride as he would have done at Downing. He'd never have done so with a horse that was not his own, so he was grateful his personal horse was currently at the Fairview stables. By the time he returned, it would be time to change for the evening anyway.

And it would be another day without talking to or spending time with Rose.

Shaking his head, Webb crossed the marble hall, heading for the stairs that would take him to the bedchambers when a commotion at the front doors caught his attention.

An older woman he had never seen was entering, escorted by a Fairview footman she leaned heavily upon, despite her colorful walking stick. Her hair was silvery-white and piled high, her turban doing nothing to cover the coif. Her lips were pursed, but her eyes darted here and there, seeming to catch every single detail they saw.

Who in the world would arrive this late to a holiday house party? Tomorrow was New Year's Eve, for pity's sake. And with a woman this frail…

Well, she wouldn't be dancing, that was for certain.

"Edith!" Lady Standhope's voice called with utter joy moments before she appeared in the hall, her arms outstretched. "I am so delighted you could spare a moment to stop by."

Webb stopped before the stairs and turned to blatantly watch this scene, wondering if the newcomer could possibly be the infamous Aunt Edith he had heard so much about.

Edith's pursed lips pursed further still as Lady Standhope approached. "Laurentia, my dear. Fairview is just as striking as I recall. A touch drafty, but in a house this size, it is to be expected." She leaned in to kiss cheeks with Lady Standhope, who only hummed at the comment.

"How long can you stay?" she asked with just as much enthusiasm as before.

Edith looked around the marble hall with a heavy sigh. "One night, perhaps two. It all depends on my niece. I am on my way to Scotland to check on dear Alden's progress, and only the good Lord knows what I will find there."

Lady Standhope patted her hand consolingly. "Have you spoken with the others?"

"Colin and Richard? Yes, yes, and I cannot speak of it yet. Believe me, I will write with the details when I can." She giggled in an almost menacing manner, which made Webb rather curious, but also a little fond of the woman.

After all, without that mischievous streak, he would never have met Rose.

"Let me show you to your room, dear," Lady Standhope insisted, flanking her friend on the other side. "I know how fastidious you are about your beds. I must have you comfortable or I shall not rest at all myself. Now, are you able to manage stairs? If not, I can make up one of the family rooms for you, it would be no trouble at all."

"I am not entirely an invalid, Laurentia," Edith snapped with a faint stomp of her walking stick. "Merely stiff from that blasted carriage. Stairs will do just fine."

Webb stepped back from the stairs to allow them full access without his involvement or intrusion.

"Ah, Lord Downing," Lady Standhope practically cooed as they reached him. "May I present Lady Edith Walker? She is our dear Miss Portman's great-aunt, you know. We are great friends, and she is going to be with us a day or two."

"A pleasure, my lady." Webb bowed respectfully, making sure to smile for effect.

Edith eyed him up and down. "You know my niece, sir?"

"I do," he confirmed, clasping his hands behind his back. "A fine woman. Quick witted and refreshingly original. She does you credit."

Edith raised one faint brow at that. "Wit and originality are not always to be praised or credited, my lord. I reserve my judgment of you until further notice." She continued up the stairs with the footman and Lady Standhope without much difficulty, her age and apparently impending death notwithstanding.

Webb was willing to bet a very great deal that Rose had no idea her great-aunt had arrived, or possibly that she would have been coming, and it seemed unfair that she should be unprepared for such a thing.

Thinking quickly, he raced towards the back of the house. He knew there was another set of stairs that led to the bedchambers there, and if he was fortunate, he would get there before the ladies would. More fortunate, even, if Edith's room were closer to the main stairs than either his room or Rose's.

These stairs came up towards the back of the corridor of rooms, where Webb was situated, but not Rose. Still, he was not hearing Lady Standhope or Lady Edith, so that was encouraging. He started down the corridor, trying to find the watercolor art of dogs at a pond that was on one side of her door. He could never remember how far down it was, and it was never more urgent than when he had something important to tell her.

He growled in frustration, tsking a little and shaking his head as he looked down the corridor. Then he stopped in his tracks.

Rose was walking towards him even now. Well, she was walking in his direction. Her eyes were lowered, her fingers were toying with a wildflower, and she did not seem to be in any way aware of where she was. And, if he was correct, she had already passed her bedchamber. Had she intended that or was she simply so distracted by whatever was going on in her mind and heart that she had missed it entirely?

He dared not hope she had been coming to seek him out. That would have been too much.

She had not seen him yet, and if she did not look up in a moment, she was going to walk right into him. That would be far too embarrassing for her, if avoiding him was the goal, and he was determined to keep her discomfort to a minimum where possible.

Webb cleared his throat very softly.

It worked. Rose looked up at once and stopped just as suddenly, her fair eyes going wide. She was pale, he noted, and a little drawn. She was lovely and exquisite even so, but it was plain to see that she was not herself. And oh, how that hurt!

"Webb," she murmured, her lips barely moving.

At least she was still calling him by his name.

He smiled as warmly as he dared. "Rose. Lost in thought?"

She nodded quickly and looked around them, her lips forming the slightest frown. "I seem to have missed my room. How embarrassing."

There was no laughter in her voice, and that frightened him most of all. She was always a little self-deprecating, and always with an air of laughing at herself, which put everyone at ease rather swiftly.

To hear her without that laughter... Well, it wasn't Rose, and Webb wasn't sure who that left.

"I've just met your aunt," he said in a light tone.

Rose's head whipped around to face him, going paler still, if it were possible. "My aunt?"

He nodded. "Great-aunt, I suppose. Lady Edith. She asked me if I knew you." He chuckled a little at the memory.

Rose did not laugh. "What did you say?" she demanded.

"The truth," he replied. When Rose stiffened, he went on. "I said you were a fine woman. Quick witted and refreshingly original. I said you were a credit to her."

If he hadn't seen it, he would not have believed it possible, but Rose's entire frame softened, seeming to sag without actually moving. "Oh, Webb…"

He'd have taken her in his arms if his legs had any power in them. As it was, he lost all feeling below his knees.

"What can I do, Rosie?" he begged her, unsure if he was asking specifically or generally, but knowing he had to ask.

A smile stretched across Rose's lips then, rather like a sunrise breaking through clouds, and he felt as though he could breathe for the first time in four days. "Rosie?" she repeated.

"Sorry," he mumbled through his own smile. "It just came out."

She tilted her head ever so slightly, a glimpse of the old Rose appearing there. "I don't mind it. From you." Then she cleared her throat and shook her head. "What can you do? Well, what did Aunt Edith say to you when you said what you did?"

Webb snorted once. "Something about wit and originality not always being praised or credited, and that she would reserve judgment on me."

Rose barked a hard laugh. "Sounds like her." She sniffled once, which was his first indication that there might have been tears somewhere. "There is nothing for you to do yet. I need to talk with her. If she has just arrived, she might not join us for supper, but I cannot say what else she may want to say or do. I must be entirely at her disposal."

"Has she come to see your progress?" Webb inquired in surprise. "I thought you were given until Twelfth Night."

"I am," Rose replied on a quick nod. "So she likely does want to know how things are going, and perhaps advise me on my task."

Webb wanted to laugh again, but he was more afraid of the task Lady Edith had put to Rose than anything else. "What will you tell her?"

Rose's mouth formed a small, wry smile, her earlier sadness returning. "I haven't the faintest idea. But...perhaps we might talk tomorrow. You and I, that is. Would that be agreeable?"

It was all Webb could do to not fall to his knees in gratitude. "Yes," he managed with all the earnestness of his soul. "Yes, tomorrow will be perfect. Is it terrible to wish you good luck?" He tried for a teasing smile.

Her wry one remained. "No, not terrible. I have a feeling I am going to need it."

CHAPTER 19

As it turned out, Aunt Edith did not send for Rose until after luncheon the next day.

It had made for a most uncomfortable evening, night, and morning.

Lady Standhope had been the one to inform Rose that Aunt Edith wished to speak with her, and she was directed to a small yellow sitting room on the east side of the house. It was one of the few rooms that Rose had not explored yet and was quite possibly the most quaint. But there was no time to properly examine it now, as Aunt Edith sat rather primly in a wingback chair, shawl around her shoulders, lace cap on her head, and dressed for a walk that Rose knew she wasn't likely to take.

It was almost military in fashion, and that certainly set a particular tone.

This was now a war council, and she was speaking with the general.

"Good day, Aunt," Rose greeted in a surprisingly timid voice. That was almost certainly going to earn comment from Aunt Edith, and she would have no defense or excuse for it.

Aunt Edith blinked and gestured to the sofa opposite. "Sit,

child."

Rose hadn't been a child in years, but the request might have been a command, and like a child, she obeyed at once. Sitting on the sofa, adjusting her skirts into a more perfect arrangement, fussing with her hair, and eventually, settling her hands into her lap, Rose met her great-aunt's eyes. There was a surprising amount of sympathy in her expression, and her mouth was not even the slightest bit pursed. "What are you doing, Rose, my girl?"

That was not the opening that she had anticipated. "What am I doing?" she repeated hesitantly. "I don't know..."

"Clearly," Aunt Edith quipped in her usual brisk tone. "If you had any idea what you are doing, you would be your usual sharp, vibrant self. But here you are, a diminishing creature of pallor and nerves. Hiding yourself away from the world and avoiding everyone and everything."

Rose inhaled sharply, less of a gasp than a painful reach for air. "How do you know that?"

Aunt Edith's look became pitying. "Did you think I would not have word from Lady Standhope before speaking with you? Letters from her as well as a very frank conversation this morning. And there are the accounts of Lady Clarke and Mrs. Richards."

"You know them as well?" Rose cried, wondering if every single person at this house party was some contact of her aunt and thus reporting on every detail regarding her.

"I do," Aunt Edith replied with a sage nod. "I did not know they would be here, but we do know each other. My point is that you are not yourself, and according to them, you were certainly yourself at the outset."

Well, there was that, at least, and Rose would have given anything not to discuss her present discomfort with her aunt. It would have been easier to talk about the marriage scheme and her lack of progress with finding a husband than try to describe her feelings.

"I was going to trick you, Aunt," Rose heard herself admit, her shoulders sagging without the weight of that burden. "I planned on making an arrangement with one of the gentlemen here to pretend to be in love with me for effect and marry me, and then we would live happily and separately for the rest of our lives, I in the cottage you bestowed and he in whatever estate he owns. It seemed easier to do that than to try and make myself likable."

"Rose," Aunt Edith scolded, almost groaning with her disapproval. "I never wanted you to make yourself anything. You are perfectly likable, in your way, and should never have to conform to someone else's ideals of how to act or be or feel. My child, did you learn nothing from my letter?"

Tears began to burn the corners of Rose's eyes and she found herself focusing on the gold buttons on her aunt's gown, shining in the daylight like some officer's uniform. "I have stopped believing I was ever going to be loved for myself. After so many years of nothing, how could I not? The proof was there before me. Never any interest from worthy suitors, and then I stopped trying so hard and began to embrace myself, and still nothing. So how could I possibly find love at one house party during two weeks? Love is not that easy for me, Aunt."

"And you believe love was easy for me, child?" She laughed one rough, almost cackling laugh. "Mr. Walker came into my life at a time when I had sworn off love and even matrimony due to my frustrations with it all, and he turned the world as I knew it on its end. Oh, it was impossible to not adore everything he did, and somehow, he found me to be much the same. I risked the scorn of my family for love of him, but I could not imagine living the dim and uninteresting version of my life one moment more. Edward breathed life into me, Rose. I hadn't been missing anything in my life at all, and then he appeared into my world, and I realized how much more there could be. And, as it happened, I gave up nothing to be with him."

"I thought your father disapproved," Rose said with a frown.

Aunt Edith smiled rather smugly. "He did. But I married him anyway, and never once felt as though something had been lost by doing so. That is what I mean by I gave up nothing. It was the easiest thing I have ever done, choosing to embrace life with Edward. Any sacrifice was worth it and rather simple, once I had made my choice. And he chose me. Every day of our lives, we chose each other, and that made all the difference."

Rose had never heard this version of Aunt Edith's story. She knew about her unpopular match with Mr. Walker, but the matter had grown less objectionable as the man's fortune had increased. No one had ever spoken of love, only of Edith's willfulness.

This changed everything Rose had ever known about her.

"So tell me now why you are avoiding that delightful Lord Downing."

Rose jerked so sharply, she actually tumbled slightly from her seat. "I beg your pardon?"

Aunt Edith sniffed a half laugh. "Lady Standhope informed me that the two of you were thick as thieves for days, and now you avoid everyone and everything. I can only presume it is he who has provoked the retreat. And you may claim that it means nothing, but that man knows the real you, my dear, and that is saying something."

"How can you possibly know that?" Rose breathed. "You spoke with him for thirty seconds."

"Told you, did he?" Aunt Edith smiled rather smugly. "I hoped he would. And as for how I know, it is quite simple. He did not tell me you were lovely or beautiful, that you were a fine

189

dancer or an accomplished musician. He did not praise your manners or graces. He said you were a fine woman, quick witted, and refreshingly original. He knows you, and praised you in the way that you would wish to be praised. You have let him get to know you, and now you are hiding from him. Am I wrong?"

Rose shook her head, her eyes filling with tears and her throat tightening. "I cannot face him. And yet…I have never hurt this much in my entire life."

"You love him," Aunt Edith overrode with a surprising gentleness. "You would not be hiding if you did not. You would know your own mind and tell him of it. The fact that you cannot face him tells me you love him and are afraid of that step."

"Yes," Rose whispered. "He is a person who feels so much, Aunt, and I am so afraid that I will not be enough if I…if I let myself…"

Aunt Edith surprised her by patting the arm of the chair beside her. "Come here, dear girl."

Swallowing tears, Rose moved to take the indicated seat and found her hand immediately clasped by her aunt. The cool, almost clammy hands encased hers with surprising warmth.

"You do not have to love him in exactly the same degrees and ways that he loves you," Aunt Edith murmured with a squeeze of her hands. "You must let him love you the way that he loves, and he must accept your love the way that you love. We all show love in different ways. It should not be a competition of whose love is truest or best or the most intense. What is important is the love, concern, and respect that is at the heart of it all."

"But what if it isn't love on his part?" Rose asked with a hitch to her voice. "What if…what if it isn't what I think, and this is all a great mistake? We are friends, Aunt, and I fear I might be so focused on matrimony and a love match that I have deluded myself."

"Love is delusional, darling," came the dry reply. "No one

who has felt it would say otherwise."

That was not a helpful response, and Rose gave her a hard look even through her tears.

Aunt Edith turned to face her more fully. "You must be brave to be vulnerable," she told Rose. "You will never be happy with yourself again if you do not tell that man how you feel, frightening though it may be. And should the worst happen, should he not return your affections, you may have the cottage anyway to hide your face and your sorrows. But you must tell him. On that I do insist."

Rose closed her eyes at this, the welling tears falling down her cheeks now. There was no comfort in the prospect of the cottage at this moment, given what she had to do to attain it. But . her aunt was right, she could not retreat forever and pretend that nothing had changed between them. Webb deserved to know how Rose felt, and Rose deserved to let her feelings be spoken, if only to know for herself that she was capable of them.

"Well?" Aunt Edith pressed with her usual air of impatience.

It would seem the heartfelt portion of this discussion was at an end.

Wiping her eyes, Rose nodded, exhaling slowly. "I will tell him. Tonight, at the New Year's Eve ball."

"Good." Aunt Edith patted her hand with more sharpness than was comforting and released her. "I will attend the dinner, but not the ball. Midnight of a new year is not pleasing at my age, only another mark against time. And I will be leaving in the morning for Scotland. I must see Alden."

Rose grimaced as she looked over her great-aunt with cautious eyes. "Can you bear such a journey? With your illness, Aunt Edith, I would hate to think…"

"I have made some improvements to the comforts in my carriage," Aunt Edith overrode with a dismissive wave of her hand. "It is quite suitable for a woman of my disposition. And I promised I would see all of you, and so I must. Now go prepare yourself for the ball while I rest. You've exhausted my energy with your problems, and I have nothing more to say." Again, she waved her hand, though her lips were curved in a very small smile.

Rising from her chair, Rose went over and kissed her aunt's chilled cheek very softly. "Thank you, Aunt Edith."

Her aunt dipped her chin in an approving nod. "You are most welcome, child. My benevolence is greater than people know, and it is high time you see it. Now good day."

Rose shook her head in amusement and left the room as instructed, her heart beginning to pound in a combination of fear and excitement. She had told Webb they would talk, and so they would. The only question remaining was how that talk would end.

It was a scant few hours later that Rose entered the ballroom at Fairview, her heart pounding as though it would actually burst through her chest and propel itself across the room. Her stays felt entirely too snug, which she knew they were not, and in her attempts to appear as lovely as possible, she felt more on display than she had in her very first Season in London.

Nothing was more important than what she was about to do, and nothing made her want to turn and run back to her bedchamber like the prospect of it. Hiding under the covers on her very comfortable bed and pretending none of this was happening was a very tempting idea. But she had promised Aunt Edith and had come to believe in the interim that her aunt was right.

She deserved this moment for herself. And she would be brave enough to be that vulnerable.

For Webb.

Biting her lip, she looked around the large space, filled with dancers and musicians, and began walking around the perimeter of the room. The Christmas décor was still on proud display, hanging until Twelfth Night, she had no doubt, and she made a careful observation of the bunches of mistletoe that had been placed in some rather surreptitious places. She was taking no chances of misunderstanding tonight, and no holiday traditions could ruin this for her.

She finally found Webb by one of the windows, surveying the dancing with a placid expression.

She took a moment to observe him before she would be seen, enjoying the warmth that filled her chest and belly, screeching out in every direction from her core just at the sight of him. His dark hair and eyes, his beautifully angled features, the hint of a smile that was always present in his lips, the lean figure he cut in such fine evening wear... Tall, dark, and handsome she had noted from their first meeting, and it still suited him now. But she would have to add to that witty, kind, mischievous, energetic, and loving. So very loving.

Could his loving nature possibly extend to her? Could Rose let him love her, if he did?

She set her hands at her stomach, the fabric of her gloves pressing against the lace overlay of her skirts. She had chosen the theme of blue and white for the evening, hoping it would enhance her eyes. Her blue satin slip beneath the lace was one of her favorites, and having that same blue satin at her bodice instead of the lace... There was a sense of armor protecting her heart with that, and the pearl details along the neckline and sleeves—as well as pearls in her hair, at her throat, and dangling from her ears— made her feel more elegant.

She wanted to be more everything right now, and the more confidence she could find in her attire and appearance, the more she might feel in her heart.

There was nothing for it now.

With shaking steps, Rose started towards Webb, holding her breath until the moment his eyes fell on her.

They widened and quickly traced the length of her. She saw his throat work, and her stomach clenched in response.

"Good evening," Rose greeted when she came to him, speaking before he could do so. "I hadn't meant to be tardy, but my hair simply would not set the way my maid and I liked. It will be just my luck if it all tumbles down on the very first dance."

Webb cleared his throat. "It looks lovely. And I wouldn't mind if it did all tumble down. I'd love to see it like that. But whatever efforts were put into your appearance tonight... Whatever you did, it was well worth it."

It was such a simple thing to say, and yet it filled Rose with such a personal delight. She took a moment, smiling just for herself, then turned to face the dancing beside him. "You look rather fine as well. A gold weskit ought to be a staple for gentlemen. It adds such refinement without being blatant."

"You're teasing me," Webb murmured. "Should I take that as encouragement?"

"Probably," Rose said with a laugh, wondering how she could possibly be laughing right now. "I've survived the meeting with Aunt Edith, and my mind feels clearer now than it has in many days."

She could feel Webb's eyes on her again, but she focused on the dance. "Good," he said softly. "I am glad to hear it." He took in a breath, held it for a moment, then exhaled in a rush. "You said you wished to talk. Should we dance to do so, or...?"

Rose shook her head, her heart moving up to her throat. The moment had come.

"I've come to a decision," she began, clasping her fingers tightly to keep them from visibly shaking.

"Have you?" Webb asked with a strange hitch in his voice.

She tried to nod, but only managed a weak swallow. "I am

giving up on the scheme. All of it. I cannot go through with it. The only person I could possibly see myself marrying here is you."

Her heart stopped at hearing his sharp intake of breath.

Hastily, she added, "And I cannot bring myself to ask you. It is too far, even for me. So if you feel anything for me, and you wish it, ask me. I'll say yes."

She had no idea if her words were even distinguishable in the rush to get them out. But they were out, and her task was done. The rest, as it were, was up to him.

"If I feel anything?" Webb put a hand at her arm, gripping surprisingly hard. "Follow me," he growled.

He moved past her and strode directly for the large marble pillars on the side of the room. She followed hard on his heels, wondering what could possibly require them to move over there.

Then he took her arm once more and pulled her behind one of the pillars. He had removed his gloves during the walk and was shoving them into the pocket of his jacket as he pressed her gently against the pillar.

He took her face in his hands, the heat of his palms against her skin making her knees shake. "Do you know how long I have felt something?" he rasped, his dark eyes almost frantically searching hers. "How many times I have talked myself in circles about feeling something? Hell's teeth, Rose, I've been in love with you for days, and so desperate for you that I wanted to break down several doors and whatever walls in my way."

Rose covered his hands with hers, sighing with a deep relief she did not know existed. "I was hiding from you," she whispered, feeling the agony of the last few days rush in on her. "I was afraid that you loved me more than I could return, and then I was afraid I was imagining it all, and—"

Webb's mouth took hers in a hot, hungry, insistent kiss that robbed her of all resistance, if not her very soul. There was no room for doubt in this kiss, and no thought but returning it with all of the unpracticed fervor she felt swirling throughout her frame.

"You imagined nothing," Webb breathed against her tingling lips. "I do love you, and I want nothing more than to marry you. But I want you to *want* to, Rose. I don't want you hiding away at Aunt Edith's cottage instead of being with me. I want to be *with* you at that cottage. Especially if it's a confined space because that sounds vastly entertaining."

Rose began to snicker at the idea, which felt utterly delicious in his hold and with his lips at such a tantalizing distance. She ventured further and kissed him fully and slowly, loving the groan it elicited from him and the shudder that raced through the arms that held her.

"I love you," Rose told him, brushing her nose against his. "And I want to marry you. I want to love you and be in love with you and choose you and…"

Webb kissed her again, hard. "You had better stop telling me what you want, Rosie," he warned in a dark, toe-tingling tone. "We're going to need a swift change of location otherwise."

They both laughed at that, holding each other as they hid from the rest of the party.

Webb pressed his lips to her brow, sighing against her skin. "So will you marry me, Rosie?"

"Yes," she vowed, sliding her hands from his to link around his neck. "And unfortunately, if we have a daughter while we're feeling so sentimental about this, we may have to name her Edith."

Webb snorted and drew Rose into his arms fully. "That's not a dreadful name. We'd just call her Edie, and no one need know that she's named for your tyrannical great-aunt who forced you into a marriage scheme at Christmas that practically propelled you into my arms."

"It would show my immense gratitude," Rose considered

with a smile, her cheek pressed against Webb's racing heart. "I'd never have found you otherwise."

He leaned back just enough to turn her face to his. "I'll name all of our daughters Edith if we're expressing gratitude for that. You've brought me back to life, Rose, and I did not even know I was gone."

Rose smiled rather dreamily and kissed him again.

Thoroughly.

Without any mistletoe in sight.

EPILOGUE

"I love this cottage. I mean it, this is exactly the sort of cottage I had hoped you would inherit."

Rose rolled her eyes heavenward as her new husband raced about Beechwood Lodge, exploring every nook and cranny. They had just arrived as part of their wedding trip, and it was the first time either of them was seeing the place. Aunt Edith had been true to her word and given Rose the cottage and stipend for it as a wedding present and encouraged her to make a trip to see it while she and Webb were enjoying some time in the Lake District during their wedding trip.

Given that they had waited until spring for the wedding, it had been easy enough to adjust their plans.

Webb, evidently, was loving that adjustment now.

Rose stripped her gloves off and laid them on the narrow table in the hall, shaking her head.

"Would madam like some tea or refreshment now that you've arrived?" inquired the kindly, soft-spoken housekeeper she'd met barely five minutes ago.

"Not yet, Mrs. Hackett. Thank you."

Mrs. Hackett nodded, still smiling. "I shall oversee the

movement of your trunks, then. Will your ladyship be requiring a separate chamber from his lordship?"

Rose had to smile at that, her cheeks warming with the now familiar heat that dwelling on her husband's nightly attentions brought her. "No, we will share. Thank you, Mrs. Hackett."

The housekeeper seemed to laugh very softly, if knowingly, and left her in the hall.

Rose removed her bonnet and shook her hair, half of it tumbling from its pins. She did not often miss that maid she'd used at Fairview, but when her hair did things like this, she tended to.

"Rosie! Rosie, you *have* to see—well, well, well..."

Rose turned to the stairs with a scolding look, knowing that tone of her husband's all too well by now. "Stop."

Webb's smile was sly and his shrug slow. "Stop what? I am only appreciating my beautiful wife, and when her hair looks like that, I want to appreciate her more."

Against her wishes, a delicious shiver of anticipation started down Rose's spine. And if the quirk to Webb's smile was any indication, he knew it, too.

She had to do something, or she'd find herself impossibly distracted for the rest of the day and into the night.

"What do I have to see, Webb?" Rose asked in as prim a voice as she could muster.

That, amazingly enough, seemed to shake him. He hurried down the rest of the stairs. "The stables! I know you said there were stables, but they are gorgeous, Rose! Can we go see them?"

He was so childlike in his enthusiasm for this place, it was as though Pierce were there with them. And seeing such a lightness in Webb was absolutely impossible to ignore, his requests impossible to deny.

"Yes, let's go," Rose decided at once. "In fact, let's ride."

Webb grinned brightly, shrugging out of his coat and

tugging off his cravat, tossing both onto the table beside her bonnet and gloves. "Absolutely. How many acres do we have?"

Her heart swelled at the word *we*, and Rose beamed at him, holding out her hand. "Thirty."

Webb took her hand and brought it to his lips as he undid the top button of his linen shirt. "Lovely. Let's stay here forever."

"We left the children in Yorkshire with your mother," Rose said with a laugh as they exited the cottage and walked towards the stables. "We'll need to get back to them eventually."

"Then let's stay here a month," came his unconcerned reply. "Or have the children brought here. Let's forget Downing House and the title and Yorkshire."

Rose laughed harder, rubbing her fingers against his fondly. "You idiot. We cannot do any of that."

Webb pulled her into his arms and kissed her, swallowing the remnants of her laughter. He cradled her face and captured her lips again and again, reigniting her hunger for him that had yet to abate in the slightest. Each kiss they shared reminded her yet again of the bliss that now filled her life and her heart, the passion she had learned she was capable of, the incomparable delight that Webb filled her days and nights with, and the sheer insanity that any of it had even come to pass.

"I love you," Rose sighed when Webb's mouth moved to her jaw, her fingers tangling in his hair.

"That's because I am kissing you senseless," he murmured as his lips dusted across her skin.

Rose chuckled once. "True. Not that I am complaining, but why?"

He groaned and kissed her throat pointedly. "Because you laughed. And I have a beastly attraction to your laugh."

It was the most ridiculous thing she had ever heard, but she pulled his head slightly away to stare directly into his dark and captivating eyes.

"What?" he asked, his intent clear.

Rose raised her brow. "We are going to the stables. Then we are going for a ride, and we are going to race."

His eyes took on a new light of interest. "Are we?"

She nodded slowly. "And whoever wins gets to decide how long we stay here. And what we do."

"I see," Webb replied as he slowly drummed his hands along her waist. "Then I only have one thing to figure out."

"Which is?"

Her husband leaned in, his brow brushing hers just as his lips moved to her ear. "If it would be more fun to win or to lose…" And then he was off and running towards the stable, his laughter echoing on the air.

Rose moaned at the unfair ploy, knowing she would have done the same thing if she'd thought of it, and turned to chase after him. "I'll get you for this, Webb Rixton!"

His only response was a series of more laughter, and Rose sighed at hearing it.

She had a beastly attraction to his laughter, too.

Win or lose, the future was bright, indeed.

*Next in the **Regency Christmas Brides** series*

Rules of a Ruse
by Laura Beers

Marriage was supposed to be the solution, but falling in love wasn't part of the plan.

Mr. Alden Dandridge has received astonishing news: he is set to inherit a thriving horse farm in a quaint Scottish village. However, there's a formidable catch- he must be married by Twelfth Night. Undeterred, Alden journeys to Scotland, convinced that a marriage of convenience will solve all his problems.

Miss Elinor Sidney has been successfully running the horse farm for the past two years, and she has no intention of relinquishing it to Mr. Dandridge. Adding to the stakes, she learns that if Alden fails to secure a bride by Twelfth Night, the horse farm will legally belong to her. When Alden enlists her help in finding a suitable bride, Elinor agrees, though she has no true intention of aiding him.

As Alden spends more time with Elinor, he comes to realize that she is the perfect solution to his predicament. He just needs to persuade her to marry him. Yet, Elinor yearns for a marriage built on love, not convenience. When someone from Elinor's past reemerges, threatening her peace, Alden knows he must risk everything- including his heart- to protect her.

Regency Christmas Brides

Four festive tales of romance.

'Twas the month before Christmas
and all through the house,
four cousins have been told they all need a spouse...

Read each of the books
in this series in any order!

A Seasonal Pursuit by Rebecca Connolly
(Rose's story)

Rules of a Ruse by Laura Beers
(Alden's story)

Yuletide Bride by Kasey Stockton
(Colin's story)

Married by Twelfth Night by Anneka R. Walker
(Richard's story)

ABOUT THE AUTHOR

Rebecca Connolly is the author of more than four dozen novels. She calls herself a Midwest girl, having lived in Ohio and Indiana. She's always been a bookworm, and her grandma would send her books almost every month so she would never run out. Book Fairs were her carnival, and libraries are her happy place.

She has been creating stories since childhood, and there are home videos to prove it! She received a master's degree from West Virginia University, spends every spare moment away from her day job absorbed in her writing, and is a hot cocoa addict.

Made in the USA
Las Vegas, NV
10 December 2024

13808026R00118